# THE BLUFF

# THE BLUFF

## A THRILLER

BONNIE TRAYMORE

*For my besties:*
*Jersey girls forever*

# CONTENTS

# ALSO BY BONNIE TRAYMORE:

*Killer Motives*

*Little Loose Ends*

*Head Case*

*The Stepfamily*

*The Guest House*

*"Nature never did betray the heart that loved her."*
William Wordsworth

# PROLOGUE

Doug Mitchell takes in the shoreline of Lake Michigan, letting his Sundancer drift around in the currents. The sight of his house high atop the bluff reminds him of what is at stake. The vote is tonight, and it's sure to be one hell of an evening. A cool wind whips up what little sand remains on the shrinking beach, and he can see the bare patch of earth where the southern stairs collapsed two years ago. But he feels safe and warm on the deck, with the soon-to-be-setting sun still overhead, beaming down on him.

It's not the same shoreline it was decades ago, but then the world is an ever-changing place. He knows this, although he doesn't let on about it to most people. Right now, his mind is drifting to another place, and he feels a delightful stirring. He pictures the curve of her back. Her slender, graceful neck. The look on her face when he makes her moan. He takes another sip of his cocktail, closes his eyes, and sinks into it.

After a few minutes, a different kind of feeling washes over him. He's dizzy. And tired. Way too tired. He's barely had one drink. He opens his eyes, and the world appears blurry. He feels clumsy. Almost immobile. Shaking his head, he tries to snap out of it, but everything's . . .

*Fuzzy.*

*Confused.*

*Off.*

He came out here alone, he thinks, although he didn't check the cabin before leaving the dock. A figure is standing on the deck now, too far away from him to make out who it is. It's someone, though, and even with his mind dulled, he knows this is not good.

Seized with panic, he struggles to pull himself out of the quagmire. Finding a last burst of strength, he attempts to spring up and go on the offensive, but his legs are like rubber. His body rocks forward a bit, accomplishing nothing.

He sinks back into oblivion as the figure approaches.

*You?*

# CHAPTER 1
## KATE

arrive five minutes late for my meeting, breathless from my run in from the parking lot. The proceedings haven't started yet. Rushing in, I whip off my scarf and coat and take a seat.

*Just in time.*

The stage is set for a contentious evening. Tonight, the town council will vote on the pressing issue of the crumbling bluff. I head up the shoreline committee, and I've been invited here this evening to present my plan, one of two the board will consider.

"Hi, Kate," the board member next to me says. "Glad you made it."

She gives my shoulder a squeeze, confirming that I've got her vote.

"Of course," I say. "Sorry, I'm late."

A tingling sensation creeps up my spine, and a feeling of dread squeezes my stomach like a vise. Perhaps it's the weather. It's early fall, but it may as well be the dead of winter. It's bitter cold and gray, with intermittent downpours.

Sheets of water batter my home at night, threatening to sweep it into the lake, and the howling wind whipping off Lake Michigan has been keeping me up. It's the same weather we were having when my husband met his untimely death a year ago, which is likely stirring up some buried feelings. A widow at forty-one. Not the way I expected my life to go when I moved here six years ago.

"The meeting of the Crest Lake Township board of directors is now in session," the president proclaims, banging his gavel with the countenance of a man desperate for power and relevance. Sam Bolger's his name.

Sam takes role, and it's lost on nobody that Doug Mitchell is absent. I fiddle with a strand of hair, twirling it between my fingers. It looks darker in this light, almost auburn. My eyes search the room, and hushed tones fill the silence as people whisper to each other.

*Where the hell is Doug?*

*Are we really going to start without him?*

*I hope he's okay.*

His allies look concerned, naturally, but even his opponents seem troubled, although that could be an act. It would be unacceptable to show their glee in the event they were feeling it. But I'm not feeling smug or excited or victorious. I'm feeling nervous. Doug is scheduled to present the opposing plan, and there's no way he would intentionally miss this meeting. His absence magnifies the gnawing feeling inside me that something is about to go terribly wrong.

Tempers have been flaring over what to do about the eroding bluff. The police had to be called during the last public hearing. There have even been a few death threats, anonymous posts and phone messages that most of us brushed off.

Silly, really. We're all on the same team, trying to fight Mother Nature. Desperate to give ourselves the illusion of control. Struggling to keep our large, lakefront luxury homes from plummeting onto the shrinking shoreline that hugs the massive body of water eighty feet below the fragile bluff.

On some level, we all know that whatever we do will only be a stop-gap in the big picture of geological time, and I can't help but wonder if that's what's making people so angry. Humanity's stubborn insistence that we can bend the planet to our will. It's obvious that we can't, and perhaps it's easier to blame each other than to face the realization that humans are at the mercy of forces we don't really understand and can no longer control.

The president seems to be stalling, fumbling with his computer as he tries to pull up the agenda and project it onto the TV screen. The board member to my right shares a theory with me. Perhaps Doug's pulling a stunt for dramatic effect, she whispers in my ear. Maybe the president's in on it—he's on Doug's side—and Doug will come bursting in at the last minute, waving some new study in his hands. After a few moments, it's clear to everyone that that's not going to happen.

Sam tables the vote for the time being and moves on to other issues. The board gets to work. There are a handful of mundane items on the agenda aside from the one that matters to me—what to do about the shoreline. I wait patiently as the board members work through other business, waiting for Doug's arrival, my palms starting to sweat. He's a board member, but I'm not.

I wonder what will happen if he doesn't show up. Will they postpone the vote, or will it go my way by default, with my proposal the only option? Item after item is addressed, and I can feel my pulse starting to race as they tick them off.

*Parcel tax proposal.*

*New library budget.*

*Changes to the vacation rental rules.*

My stomach is in knots now. If the vote goes my way, it will be a Pyrrhic victory, inflicting massive economic consequences on my lakefront neighbors. Doug's plan to simply shore up the bluff at the toe, the spot where the waves hit and wear it down, is the simple one. The less expensive one. It's got the environmental groups up in arms, though. They've grown increasingly vocal over the last few years.

The environmentalists want to force the removal of all existing seawalls, like the one Doug Mitchell installed in front of his home, and ban all such structures. Let nature take its course. Force lakefront owners to move back their homes or demolish them if they are in danger of falling off the bluff. But none of them are on the shoreline committee, and none are on the board. They'll be upset whichever way it goes tonight.

My plan is a compromise of sorts. If I win, there will be consequences. Expensive ones that will dramatically reduce some people's property values and limit beach access for everyone. And lots of visceral anger, much of it directed at me, especially from my wealthy lakefront neighbors, who will absorb most of the cost. Several million dollars, split between ten of us. Sweat beads form at my temples as the minutes tick along to the rhythm of the cheap wall clock mounted above my seat.

*Why do they keep it so hot in here?*

The council meets at the town center, a small, institutional structure that used to serve as a middle school. The chairs are small and uncomfortable. I sit up and twist from side to side, trying to stop my lower back from cramping up. After an hour or so, there's nothing left on the agenda but the bluff, and I'm wondering if they'll postpone my presentation and the vote.

A knock at the door startles us.

*Police*, a voice calls out.

The door opens, and a young officer enters tentatively, crouching his way into the room. It's a tight community, and he's likely a bit intimidated. We're a powerful bunch. If he ran into one of us around town, I imagine he'd be deferential. But this isn't a coffee shop or a grocery store, and this isn't a social call.

After a moment, he straightens up, and his face registers the requisite look of authority. "Doug Mitchell's been reported missing," he says. "He went out on his boat earlier today and never returned. The Coast Guard is conducting a search."

My stomach sinks. I'm sure I've turned a shade paler. Gasps echo around the room. We all sit with the shocking news for a few moments as the officer bites his lower lip.

He continues. "We're going to need to interview all of you. Detective Whittaker is on his way. Please stay seated and be patient."

With that, the vote is delayed.

———

Travis Whittaker leans back in his chair, eyeing me. I can see tension lines on the detective's forehead. He seems to have aged since I last saw him, although his thick, dark head of hair reveals few strands of gray. It's his eyes. They look heavy and full, like the weight of the world sits behind them.

He's been working his way through the group, and I'm second-to-last. It would have been better to get it over with. Waiting around only increased the tension. Nobody knew what to say to each other, so nothing but awkward silence filled the space between us as we stood in the hallway, waiting for our turns to go in and be interviewed.

"So, Ms. Breslow. You arrived five minutes late," he says.

"I just said that," I reply, immediately regretting my sharp tone.

The detective's nostrils flare ever so slightly. He's an attractive man for his age—early fifties—with a neatly trimmed beard and dark, steely eyes. Right now, though, he looks menacing.

"Yes. I was about five minutes late," I say in a softer tone. My throat feels as if it's about to close up on me.

He narrows his eyes on me, and I look away. I catch myself absent-mindedly stroking my neck and stop myself, placing my hands on the tabletop.

*This feels all too familiar.*

"And why were you late?"

"The rain," I offer. "It got heavy when I was driving down Lakeside." Tapping my fingers on the tabletop, I search for something to add. "I had to drive more slowly."

He nods and jots something down on his notepad. Almost everyone at the meeting had to drive down that road in the rain. It's not a very good excuse, but it's all I can give him.

"Did Doug Mitchell give you any indication that he was planning to miss the meeting tonight?" he asks.

"No, not at all," I reply. "We were all shocked when he didn't show up tonight."

"Have you heard from him today?" he says.

I shake my head no.

"When's the last time you had any contact with him?" he asks.

I look off to the side, struggling to keep myself focused and calm. I turn back to him. "In person?"

"In general," Whittaker replies.

"We've been on the same email and text chain over the last week or so. Exchanging information in anticipation of the vote."

"You didn't answer my question."

I swallow. He's already seen our text stream, I assume. "Yesterday. Around seven in the evening."

"Was that an email or a text?"

"It was a text."

"What did it say?"

I pull up my phone, hold it in my palm, and let him read the exchange. His eyes rest on my last line to Doug Mitchell.

**If you do that, I'll bury you.**

It would have been less stressful for me if Whittaker's face had registered some kind of surprise. Instead, he closes his notepad and puts his pen down. I struggle to keep a neutral look on my face. Then he informs me that I can leave and asks me to send in the next board member.

I start for the door, but then turn back to him. "In paperwork," I offer. "I meant I'd bury him in paperwork." Then I turn away again and continue to the door.

"Don't leave town," he calls out. "We're sure to have more questions as the investigation develops."

I nod and keep walking.

As my car winds up the dark, curvy, tree-lined road to my lakefront home, I struggle to steady my shaking hands. This night already had me on edge, and I can feel my pulse racing as I reach the bend in the road near the top. The part where the drop-off is the steepest. They replaced the guardrail with another one that looks exactly the same as the last one, which proved to be inadequate.

*What was the point of that?*

Sometimes, I can ignore it and drive right past. On sunny days, when the sky is bright and the birds chirp and all is well in the universe. It looks so different in the daylight. But tonight is foggy and foreboding, and I drive slowly. So slowly, I'd probably get a ticket if an officer was behind me. I don't look to my right, though, because then I have to picture it. And imagine the look of terror on my husband's face as he plunged through the rail and over the side.

*What was he thinking?*

*Or was he not thinking at all?*

*Did he scream?*

*Or was there no time?*

A chill runs up my spine as I turn carefully around the bend and breathe a sigh of relief. Sometimes, I get the sensation that he's in the car with me, and I can almost feel his breath on my neck.

Now, Doug is missing, and I have no idea what to do next or what this means for me and my shoreline plan. All I know is I have to sell my house and get out of this town before I lose my mind.

*Or worse.*

# CHAPTER 2
## TRAVIS

"Travis! Are you with me?"

Sloane's sharp tone snaps Travis out of his stupor. He gives his head a vigorous shake. "Sorry, Sloane. What were you saying?"

Then he stands and starts to pace around the precinct.

*Get the blood moving.*

"I was saying that it doesn't make any sense," she repeats.

Travis nods, his eyes heavy, in need of sleep. Sloane's a newlywed, just back from her honeymoon, so he waited until this morning to call and bring her up to speed, giving her one last night of peace. He tossed and turned, waiting for news on the search and rescue, and maybe got an hour or two of sleep before giving up, driving to the precinct, and starting on the case. Although Doug Mitchell's death hasn't been ruled a homicide yet, he's pretty sure it will be.

*Soon.*

And he told her so right before he got distracted, reflecting on the last homicide case they worked on just over a year ago. The one that's still unsolved. It's been on his mind lately, and now he worries that the cases might be related. He's getting ahead of himself, he knows, but that's his way.

"What doesn't make any sense?" he asks Sloane.

Sloane Davis is the other detective for Crest Lake Township. And his partner, sort of. They normally divide up the cases, except when the case is a high-profile felony. One that requires lots of man hours, like this one is sure to be.

"That one of his neighbors would kill him over the vote," she repeats.

"I didn't *say* that one of his neighbors killed him over the vote," he says, a little sharper than he intended.

Sloane's eyes widen, and she gives him that look. The one that tells him to watch it.

"I didn't mean for it to come out like that." He throws up his hands. "Forgive me?"

"Don't I always?" She looks him up and down. "You need to get your beauty sleep, Whittaker. You look like hell."

He shrugs.

*She's right.*

*I look like hell.*

She, on the other hand, looks radiant. Fresh from her honeymoon in St. Barts, with her tawny complexion all a glow and her dazzlingly white smile even brighter than he remembers. A young Halle Berry. Travis is nearly old enough to be her father, and he doesn't think of her like that. It's merely an observation. She doesn't look like the kind of woman who would choose to carry a gun and examine crime scenes for a living. More like a high-powered attorney or the CEO of a public relations firm, and he often wonders if she was pushed into the decision or if it was her own. Her father is a legend of sorts in their business over in the Detroit area.

"I didn't get much sleep last night. This case might be bigger than we think."

"Aren't you getting a bit ahead of yourself, Travis?"

"Just trying to cover all the bases," he replies. "You were saying that it doesn't make any sense that his neighbors would be angry with him. Care to elaborate?" he asks.

"More of the neighbors were upset about the opposition plan, not Doug Mitchell's plan. His was the modest one. It seems more likely that one of them would go after Kate Breslow and her allies. Her plan's got a much bigger price tag."

"Unless it's one of the radical groups," Travis offers. "Mitchell's sea wall is far worse for them."

"Their bark is usually worse than their bite."

"Not always," he says. "Colorado? In ninety-eight?"

He's referring to a sensational arson attack by a radical eco-terrorist group that caused twenty-six million dollars in property damage in Vail. They later went on to firebomb a University of Washington research facility.

"They usually target property, not people."

"Tree spiking could kill a person."

"But it hasn't," she says.

"*Yet*," he adds. "The board members have gotten death threats, Sloane. And we've got two dead bodies, one on each side of the issue. Ryan Breslow and now Doug Mitchell. There's that new environmental group, too. The Shoreline Liberation Front."

"Okay, well. What do we know so far?" she asks.

Travis gives her the rundown. Doug Mitchell's body was found in the lake around three o'clock in the morning after nearly twelve hours of searching. His wife, Claudia, arrived back home early that afternoon and found her husband missing. He'd left around eleven that morning to take the boat out for a spin to clear his head, something he often did.

"She started to get nervous when he wasn't back by late afternoon. It had started to rain. They'd planned to have an early dinner before he went to the meeting. She couldn't reach him on his cell, so she called the police. And when they realized the boat was still out, they alerted the Coast Guard. They did a grid pattern search and found the body. About eight feet under water."

"That was fast," Sloane says.

"They got lucky, I guess. He wasn't too far out, and the water's not too cold yet."

Cold water forces bodies to sink further into the depths of the lake and stay down longer because it halts the decomposition, which causes them to rise. Consequently, each May, as the ice melts and the water warms, they get their seasonal slew of dead bodies washing up on shore. Most are accidents. People falling off while fishing or imbibing out on the lake, all alone. Once in a while, though, they catch a homicide. That months-long delay in finding the body can help a person get away with murder.

*Not this time, though.*

"Seems pretty convenient," Sloane remarks. "He magically falls off a boat and disappears in time to stop the vote?"

"Yup." Travis pulls on his beard. "My thoughts exactly."

"Where's the boat?"

"They haven't found it yet."

"Odd," she says. "What does he have?"

"A cruiser. Sundancer three-twenty."

"It didn't just vanish," she says.

"It could," he says.

"Not on a night like that," she says.

At thirty-five feet long, the Sundancer 320 is a midsize cruiser, and much larger vessels have fallen victim to the lake's wrath. But Sloane's right. Not in the kind of weather they were having on the night Doug Mitchell's body was found. It was raining on and off, but the wind had died down. And it's the wind that whips up the waves and makes trouble.

"You know what else is odd?" she asks.

He has a feeling he knows where she's going with this, but he plays along. "No. What?"

"Kate Breslow happens to be at the center of a homicide investigation. *Again.*" Her brows rise as she eyes him.

He knows what she's insinuating with her Kate Breslow comment, but he plays Devil's advocate. "It's a small town," he offers.

"Not that small."

They both sit with the information for a few moments in comfortable silence. Sloane takes a sip of her designer coffee. Probably a latte. She's got expensive taste. And Travis takes a swig of the dark roast she brought for him, grateful that he could dump the cup of office swill he'd been choking down before she arrived.

Ryan Breslow's car veered off a cliff about a year ago as he was driving up Lakeside Avenue on a rainy night, washing away any potential evidence of another car in the vicinity. His car had been smashed to bits, along with his body, so there was little to work with in terms of evidence of another car crashing into him. He and Sloane figured that someone came at him head-on, maybe a drunk driver. Crossed over the center line. Sent him over the edge in a knee-jerk attempt to avoid a head-on collision and then fled the scene in a panic.

Kate Breslow's alibi was sketchy, and he'd always felt that

she was hiding something. They went out to dinner the night it happened, and they'd met at the restaurant. But she hadn't given a good explanation as to why they'd driven separately and why he went home without her. Her GPS had verified what she said. She was in another part of town when it happened. Claimed that she needed to stop at a friend's house.

It seemed odd to him that she would do that after a date night, and he wondered if they'd had some kind of argument at dinner. The timeline they'd constructed wasn't perfect, and some other loose ends didn't quite add up. Oddly, the victim's mother didn't seem too eager to get to the bottom of it; Breslow's father was deceased. His mother seemed content to believe that her son died in a tragic accident, which was a point in the wife's favor.

At the time, they assumed another driver was involved. Unless Ryan Breslow had a death wish, it seems unlikely that he would have driven his car off a cliff, although his wife revealed that he'd had a few drinks that night, which was confirmed by the waiter at the restaurant. If it wasn't the wife, they assumed it was unintentional, with the other driver leaving the scene.

No video has surfaced yet, and the case is still open. Technically, Breslow's manner of death was ruled undetermined, leaving the door open to a prosecution if any information should come to light. But Travis and Sloane consider it to be an unsolved homicide. But now that another person involved in the shoreline revitalization issue has turned up dead, Travis is rethinking it. Maybe someone tried to run him off the road intentionally. Someone could have come up from behind and forced him over the edge.

"The deaths could be connected," Sloane says.

"Now, who's getting ahead of herself? The Mitchell case hasn't even been ruled a homicide yet." Travis smirks.

Sloane's propped up on her elbow, staring off into space, his attempt at levity having fallen flat. After a few minutes, she turns to him. "For real, Travis. What do you think?" she asks.

"It crossed my mind."

"And? What's your gut telling you?" she asks.

He shrugs. "Too early to tell."

Travis decides to keep his thoughts to himself for now so as not to taint her powers of analysis.

"And yours?"

"Off the top of my head? Two dead husbands? I'd say femme fatale."

*And now she smiles.*

# CHAPTER 3
## KATE

t crosses my mind that this might not be the wisest course of action, but it's too late to change my mind. Because Claudia Mitchell just peeked out of her living room window and spotted my car in her driveway. Two days have passed since they found Doug's body, and I feel compelled to stop over. Bring a casserole. It's what people do.

The Mitchells live two houses down from me, one of ten lakefront homeowners in Crest Lake, and our relationship hasn't exactly been warm and fuzzy over the last few years. The house between us is owned by Sam Bolger, the town council president, but he operates it as a vacation rental, as do several others on our block. I've had a hard time making friends here, with so many transient occupants.

Claudia is nearly a decade older than me. Although she wears it well, the difference in age is still noticeable. The few times we've socialized, trying to be neighborly, I could tell it bothered her. *Oh, wait until you hit fifty*, Claudia said at one of our earlier gatherings, warning me of things to come: dark circles, hot flashes, sagging jowls. I'm sure that Claudia's had some freshening up. She looks great, but she still seems threatened by me.

Then there are the subtle digs at my childlessness. *Well, it's easy to have a body like yours when you haven't birthed two hearty boys.* Yes, she has me there. Although I've never really felt the maternal urge, I've always reserved the option. Now, motherhood seems unlikely, and I feel a pang of loss in my gut as I think about what might have been.

Grabbing the casserole dish from the passenger seat, I head over to her front door. It's the right thing to do. Plus, I'm anxious for more information. I've been on edge since the meeting. There's been no further news about Doug, and I need to know what happened. I have no idea if his death has been ruled a homicide or an accident.

*Should I be expecting another call from Detective Whittaker?*

If so, better to get ahead of it, even if it will mean an awkward interaction with Claudia Mitchell. Their home is large and grand, and even closer to the edge of the bluff than mine. It's an older Tudor-style home, dark brown and formal, that looks a bit out of place among the more recently constructed contemporary craftsman and farmhouse structures. It's been in Claudia's family for a few generations.

Claudia steps out the screen door onto her stoop and folds her arms across her chest. "Kate Breslow," she says flatly. "To what do I owe the pleasure?"

"Hi, Claudia," I reply. "I'm sorry for your loss." That sounds trite, but I can't think of anything better to say.

She nods.

*So far, so good.*

"I brought you a little something." I hold out the casserole dish, and Claudia takes it from me.

"Trying to finish me off too?" Claudia eyes me with the hint of a smile on her face.

Although I'm not exactly known for my culinary prowess, it was an unnecessary dig. I'm starting to simmer, but I force my face into a polite smile.

"Can we not, Claudia? Please?"

Claudia takes a deep breath as she holds out the casserole dish in front of her.

*A buffer zone.*

"What do you want, Kate?" she asks.

"Nothing. I only wanted to pay my respects."

Claudia rolls her eyes. "Thanks, I guess." She shrugs.

"Have you gotten any news?" I ask.

"So that's what this is? A fact-finding mission?" Her jaw stiffens.

"No! My God, Claudia. Why do you have to be so difficult all the time? We both lost our husbands. We're neighbors. Why can't we just . . ." I take a deep breath.

"What? Be *friends?*" Claudia scoffs.

"I'm not your enemy," I offer.

"You know your plan completely screws us over, Kate!"

"It's the best plan all around, Claudia. In the long run. Even Doug was coming around to that."

Claudia's nostrils flare. "You don't know anything about my husband or what he was or wasn't coming around to. You're not fooling me with your holier-than-thou act about what's best for everyone. You're out for yourself, like the rest of us. And I'm going to fight you. You think you won, but you didn't. This isn't over."

"I guess we'll see about that," I reply.

She narrows her eyes on me. "You need to go, Kate. *Now.*"

With that, I turn and head back to her car, my neighborly visit having backfired completely.

———

Sitting out on my deck, I take in the lake in front of me. A lake that's more like an ocean, with all the danger, adventure, and intrigue that suggests. A lake that can swallow tankers and airplanes whole, never to be seen again. A lake that can spawn a twenty-foot tsunami. But when the sun is setting, and the light reflects magically off the tranquil water, bathing it in pastel hues, it's hard to believe. This is one of those evenings.

Fluffy purple clouds hover over streaks of yellow, orange, and magenta, lighting up the sky. The lake's shimmering, glassy surface meets up with it at the horizon, concealing its depths and dangers. The sharp, sweet chirps of the robins and bluebirds fill the air. Happy sounds, but with an undercurrent of desperation in their cries, as if the creatures know this is the calm before the storm.

The air is cool but not frigid. Fall can be like that. A hint of summer one day, the dead of winter the next. I take stock of my life, thinking about where to go from here. Selling this house, getting out of this town. That's what I want now. My roots here aren't very deep. The recent past is filled with tragedy. If the vote goes my way, I'm sure to have a host of enemies.

*Where would I go?*

*Back to New York?*

I had a life there once.

Before I met the man who changed the trajectory of my life.

The ringtone on my cell pulls me out of the daydream. It's the council president, Sam Bolger. I'm tempted to let it go to voicemail, but I decide to answer. Sam fills me in on the investigation. Nothing yet about Doug, he says.

"We're doing a re-vote next week," he informs me.

I'm pretty sure I have the votes for it to go my way, but then you never know. With Doug's death, things could change.

"Oh, and Gavin Mitchell will serve out the rest of Doug's term. He'll be coming to the vote next week."

"But he doesn't even live here!" I protest. Now I understand what Claudia meant. *This isn't over*, she said. Because her son, the attorney, is coming to the rescue. What a disaster. He's a major mama's boy, too. This isn't good news for me.

"He's moved back. To support his mother during this difficult time. I'm sure you can understand. We felt it was best to agree to her request that he replace Doug," Sam says.

I say what I'm expected to say.

*Of course.*

*I understand.*

But I wonder.

Is this really a difficult time for Claudia?

Or is she happy to be free of him?

Sam's another longtime resident with deep roots in the area, but while Claudia's family is old-money Chicago, Sam comes from generations of farmers. He owns a sizable percentage of the blueberry business, along with some tree farms. He also owns a few of the undeveloped lots around the lake, as well as the home he lives in on the southern end of our street; he's one of the few wealthy farmers in town to join in the lakefront development boom. He was staunchly team Doug, so it doesn't surprise me that he's backing Gavin as a replacement. I've got some work ahead of me if I want to pass my plan.

With the call ended, I pull a blanket tightly around myself, my knees tucked up into a cocoon. A chill is coming in off the lake. The wind has picked up, and the leaves rustle in the background, warning of what's to come. The faint scent of burning wood wafts over to me from a neighbor's house.

*A fire would be nice tonight.*

I should head in soon. Dangerous gusts come out of nowhere, and I don't want a tree branch falling on my head. This time of year, the wind can get so strong that I have to lean into it with all my weight to take a step forward toward the lake. Some mornings I awake to find my porch furniture scattered all over the lawn. I have to admit the raw power of nature is intoxicating. I've never seen anything quite like it and being this close to it has its moments.

I take a sip of my herbal tea and sigh. There's nothing for me here anymore, and I want desperately to sell this place and leave. But I can't. Not until we do something about the eroding bluff. A new buyer wouldn't even be able to get insurance, and my life savings are in this house.

Where would I go if I could sell this place? The idea of moving back to New York is tempting. After half a decade in this claustrophobically small town, I crave the anonymity of a city. The random adventures that await around every corner.

Would it be the same in my forties, though? With everyone married? Raising kids? Most of the people I knew have moved to the suburbs. Perhaps I'm pining for my youth or what might have been if I hadn't met Ryan Breslow.

I remember the day he poked his head into my classroom like it was yesterday. I wore navy slacks and a white blouse with matching polka dots. Ryan was in jeans and a tan pullover. It was his eyes that really got me. Crystal blue and bright. I'd never seen eyes that color, and I wondered if he wore tinted contacts. The floppy-haired, surfer-dude look didn't match his confident demeanor. Perplexing yet intriguing.

*A student?*

Could be. He looked about my age. Mid-thirties. It was an evening class, so my students were of all ages. He seemed too confident to be a student, yet a bit informal for an instructor, even at The New School. One of those hip professor-types, maybe? The kind that liked to get chummy with students?

"I'm looking for room three-twelve," he said.

His voice was like velvet. Deep and soothing. It stirred something in me, somehow sounding familiar, as if my entire life had been leading up to that moment. Then he smiled. A boyish smile tempered by a thin layer of manly stubble, and my stomach did a little flip. Nothing like that had ever happened to me before.

"Oh, it's around the corner," I replied. "Let me show you."

I walked to the doorway, where he stood, and started to explain. The room numbers on the floor didn't make sense, I told him. They went up and then down again. I pointed him in the right direction. Then he placed a hand on my shoulder, and I felt a little surge of electricity.

"Thanks," he said.

He introduced himself as Ryan Breslow.

Photographer.

Filling in for a friend as a guest speaker.

I revealed that I was a child life specialist teaching a child development class.

"What's a child life specialist?" Ryan asked.

He leaned closer to me, his arms folded across his chest,

pulling me into his orbit. I backed away, a little freaked out by the effect he was having on me.

"Class is starting soon." I motioned to the students making their way around the two of us and entering the classroom.

"Would you like to grab a drink after class? It's not fair to leave a guy hanging."

*And that was how it all began.*

Was it fate or a simple random occurrence? Ryan popping into my class? I'm not particularly dogmatic about these things, but at the time, it had a movie-level meant-to-be feeling. It was intoxicating, and I went with it. And before I knew it, he was whisking me off to Michigan, and I was no longer Kate Sullivan.

# CHAPTER 4
## KATE

A thundering crash startles me out of my reminiscence. My heart is immediately in my throat. I jump up, my eyes darting around for clues, and the unmistakable sound of glass shattering into a million pieces still rings in my ears.

I will myself to calm down.

*It's the wind.*

*A tree branch, maybe.*

*It's nothing.*

But a chill permeates my bones, nonetheless. I've not told a soul about this, but I've had a strange feeling lately. Like someone is watching me, even when I'm securely inside the house. Sometimes I startle, as if he's still here, lurking around a corner.

I've never been one to believe in ghosts. I'm a woman of science. I tell myself it's the loneliness. The sadness. The guilt, causing my mind to play tricks on me. If I'm being honest, though, I've felt something.

*A presence?*

*Or was it an angry adversary?*

*Lurking in the shadows?*

Calling 9-1-1 seems like overkill, but then I think about the threats, especially the latest one, attached to a thread in a local news article.

**I know where you live.**

I grab my phone, punch in 9-1-1, lock myself in the downstairs bathroom with a kitchen knife, and wait. My heart races as I think about who might be out in my living room. I know we've had some burglaries in the neighborhood lately, and that would be preferable to someone coming after me about the bluff. Doug's dead, and although it could very well be an accident, it seems like too big of a coincidence for that to be the case.

I try not to panic. I tell myself it was a tree branch, and I hope for the best. In a few short moments, the officer and I will be laughing about it, chalking it up as a silly misunderstanding. Just in case, I clench the knife tightly in my fist and hold it up, ready to strike.

———

Did you notice anything before the crash?" he asks.

It's the same young officer who came to our meeting. Matt Alverson's his name. Light brown hair. Thin, but on the taller side. Respectful, and maybe a little insecure. The kind of officer who will probably grow nicely into his position. I'm comforted by the fact that he's not on a power trip.

"No, I don't think so."

"Are you sure?" he asks.

When I think back, I remember hearing the leaves rustling across the grass. I thought it was the wind, but it could have been a person. I explain this to the officer, and he nods, jotting this down on his notepad.

A brick sits on my living room floor, a carpet of glass shards covering the hardwood surface, so obviously, someone was on my property. He searched the house and found nobody. I did a quick inventory of my valuables. Nothing appears to be missing. We combed through video footage from the two cameras that cover the front and back main entrances, but there was nothing. It's as if the perpetrator knew where the cameras were and avoided them.

"What do we do from here?" I ask.

"I'll take the brick, and they'll test it for prints," he says.

"I'm totally exposed here now," I say, glancing over at the gaping hole that used to be covered with glass. "Are you going to call Detective Whittaker?"

"We don't usually get them involved in acts of vandalism."

"My husband was killed last year. Doug Mitchell is dead. What if this is connected somehow?"

The last thing I want is an evening filled with Whittaker and his relentless questioning, but perhaps this could be a good thing for me. I know he has doubts about me regarding what happened to my husband. I was the beneficiary of his life insurance policy, and they always look at the spouse. Perhaps now he'll see me as a victim.

"Okay." He nods.

With the windowpane missing, a winter chill ripples through the living room.

I motion to the fireplace. "Let me get that started. Seems like we're going to be here a while."

———

Soon after Whittaker arrives, Officer Alverson tells us he needs to get going. It's not a high crime area, but the department is understaffed, he explains. He's spread thin, and he needs to patrol the town.

"I've got it," Whittaker assures him.

I go over it twice, and thankfully, the detective's demeanor is different this time. *As it should be.* I'm the victim tonight, after all.

"Have you learned anything more about Doug Mitchell's death?"

His brows rise. "I can't comment on an ongoing investigation," he says.

I like the fact that he's been knocked off balance a bit by my directness. I decide to go on the offensive.

"What if this is somehow connected to Doug's death? And to my husband's death? Speaking of which, have you made any more progress on my husband's case?"

"We're working on it."

I roll my eyes. "I've been hearing that for over a year now."

"Let's focus on tonight, shall we?"

We go over some of the threats that the town council members have received. They're all over the place, literally. Some threads attached to local news articles, like the one directed at me. A few messages were left on the town council answering machine. Nothing on my cell phone, or anyone else's, as far as I know, which is why we hadn't taken them very seriously.

"Your husband and Doug Mitchell were on opposite sides of the issue, correct?"

"Yes."

*He knows this.*

*Why is he asking again?*

"Can you walk me through your husband's position once more?"

I take a deep breath and force myself to go through it again without an attitude.

"Ryan wanted to let nature take its course. Push back the property lines for those of us on the lakefront. Ban what he liked to call 'hard armor.' Remove all existing structures. Similar to the Chikaming plan, but without the option to use sandbags or geo-tubing."

I'm referring to Chikaming Township, a lakefront town on the southern border of the state, where they adopted a similar plan. Even with the concession of sandbags and geo-tubing to slow erosion, which my husband wanted to eliminate, the plan had evoked the ire of many lakefront property owners and many beachgoers.

"A hard armor ban would include revetments?"

"Yes. In Ryan's mind, he didn't see a distinction."

"And what about in your mind?"

My plan is a compromise, and he knows this. Now my heart is starting to race.

*Is he trying to trip me up?*

"As you know, I don't consider revetments to be the same as constructing a sea wall. Revetments have openings to let the water and sediment ebb and flow more naturally. My plan involves constructing a revetment and reangling the bluff. But my plan is much more expensive, and it will take up more beach space because a revetment needs to be angled, like the bluff."

"So, you don't consider revetments to be hard armor?"

"I try to avoid that term. It's political."

"Let me put it another way. You consider revetments to be a good solution, and your husband disagreed?"

I swallow. "Yes. I suppose that's true."

"So, at the time of his death, you and your husband were not in agreement about the shoreline?" he asks.

"You could say that. But we agreed to disagree, if you know what I mean. We didn't discuss it much."

My stomach lurches as I think back, trying to recall if there was any public evidence at odds with what I told him.

"And what about Doug Mitchell? What did he think about revetments?"

"Doug wasn't opposed to revetments, in general. He was against reangling the bluff because it would take away another twenty feet of their property and eliminate the beach in front of his house. It would also reduce beach access for the public. Their property line is closest to the edge, so if my plan were adopted, it would affect them the most. They'd have to move their house back. His plan was to construct a seawall across the stretch of beach in front of our homes like he had. He and Claudia were confident that the water would recede naturally over time as it has over the decades."

"And if Ryan had pushed through a plan to ban hard armor? How would that have affected Doug Mitchell's property?"

"It would have been catastrophic for them, especially if they were forced to remove their seawall. One bad storm could potentially cause a collapse."

This wasn't an exaggeration. Ryan had photos of the bluff from fifteen years ago when he bought the home. At the time, the slope was gentler. Much less dangerous. Now, it's almost a straight-up vertical wall. All ten of us on the lakefront have lost chunks of property. The public stairs leading down to the beach collapsed a few years back. They slid right down the crumbling bluff, killing one person.

Whittaker nods, jotting something down on his notepad. He looks up at me again. "Have you heard of the Shoreline Liberation Front?"

"I, um, yes. I believe Ryan mentioned them to me." I catch myself fiddling with my necklace and quickly lower my hand.

It's not lost on Whittaker.

*Damn it.*

"Was he involved with them?" Whittaker asks.

"I think so, although he never actually came out and told me so. We didn't talk about it much before he . . ." I look away and then back at him. "Before my husband was killed. As I said, we'd agreed—"

"To disagree. Yes. So you said." Whittaker keeps his eyes trained on me, and it feels like he can read my mind, forcing me to look away.

It's not a lie, but not exactly the whole truth. Ryan was furious with me for going public with my proposal, and I know for a fact that Ryan was involved with that group. He may have even founded it, for all I know. But if I tell the detective that I knew about his involvement, he might figure out what else I uncovered, and that wouldn't be good for me.

It makes me sick to think about all the deception. Even I didn't know everything, and it's something I want to move past, not dwell on tonight. I'm not giving Whittaker anything, either. If Ryan was involved, he has to do his job and dig it up on his own.

"How's your relationship with the Mitchells?" he asks.

"They weren't happy about my plan. Aside from that, it was fine."

His head cocks to the side as he eyes me. "Claudia Mitchell told me you stopped by earlier today."

"Yes. I dropped off a casserole. Paid my respects."

"She claims you were pumping her for information."

I let out a huff. "Is this an interrogation, Detective? Should I call my attorney?"

"Not at all. I'm simply trying to figure out who might have it in for you."

I roll my eyes. "I don't see Claudia Mitchell throwing a brick through my window, if that's what you're getting at."

"Do you have any other enemies? Unrelated to the bluff issue?"

"Nobody in particular. I'm sure you know about the threats we've gotten as a group," I remind him. "The ones that have been left at the office or attached to some of the news articles."

"Right. Well, if you think of anyone, let me know."

I nod.

"Do you have somewhere you can stay tonight until you can get that fixed? I can have a squad car come by a few times, but I can't have someone here outside your home all night."

There's only one person I feel comfortable calling who would be willing and able to take me in at nine in the evening, although I'm not crazy about the idea of staying at her house.

"Yes," I say. "I suppose there's one person I could call. You think that's necessary?"

He shrugs. "My gut says no. The brick is likely a scare tactic by one of the radical groups. They don't normally go after people. But then, you never know. There's always the chance of a rogue lone wolf. Better safe than sorry."

"Do you think this is connected to what happened to my husband? Or Doug?"

"In my experience, killers don't usually give warnings," he says. "They just kill. And the Mitchell case has yet to be ruled a homicide."

"Right."

"Even if no murderer is roaming about, you're still vulnerable to a burglary, with that windowpane missing. They've been on the uptick lately."

"Thanks for the warning," I say.

A hint of compassion emanates from his eyes for once. Maybe this incident is a good thing. Perhaps he'll finally lay off me.

"A woman living alone in this big house with no alarm? I'd install one if I were you."

"Good idea. I'll check into that tomorrow right after I get someone on the window repair."

As we wrap things up and I close the door behind him, my mind flashes back to my life in New York City. My doorman building. The three deadbolts I methodically engaged each time I closed my apartment door behind me.

When Ryan talked me into moving here, he sold it as a safe place. A place where you could leave your doors unlocked. A place where children could roam freely around the neighborhood. But right now, as I look around my large, empty home, I realize I felt safer in the city, with neighbors so close they could hear me scream.

*Who would hear me scream in here?*

# CHAPTER 5
## KATE

Margaret Brenner fusses over me like a mother hen, fluffing my bed pillows as if I'm a child. And I must admit, it feels nice. Margaret's a widow, decades older than me. Not a lakefront owner, but a longtime towny with a pleasant grandma face and a stout, sturdy stance. The kind of woman who could chase away a burglar with a rolling pin covered in flour.

"Will you be warm enough, dear? Do you need an extra blanket?"

"I'll be fine, Margaret. Thank you," I assure her.

In fact, it's baking hot in the house, and I'll likely need to crack the window a bit when Margaret leaves to get some air circulating in this stuffy room.

"It's terrible how this issue is ripping the town apart. Do you want some more tea?" she asks.

I woke Margaret when I called a little after nine in the evening. As I suspected, she had been willing and even eager to have me come over and stay. She's lonely, with her only daughter living overseas and her husband long gone.

"I'm okay, thanks." I bring the porcelain teacup, razor-thin with tiny flowers and a delicate gold rim, to my lips. I take a last sip of my lukewarm chamomile tea, feeling grateful that I have a safe place to stay tonight.

"Need anything stronger? You must be so shaken up, Kate," she says.

"Oh, no. I'm fine, thanks. It's probably nothing. Just a silly act of vandalism."

"It's not nothing. Look what happened to your husband. And Doug."

"Whittaker thinks it's unlikely to be connected to the brick. Killers don't normally give warnings, he pointed out." I shrug.

Margaret tilts her head to one side and purses her lips. "Hmm. I suppose that makes sense. Is Travis Whittaker still giving you a hard time? That burns me up. It's because you're not from around here. People can be like that with newcomers."

I've been here for half a decade, and I hardly consider myself a newcomer. Perhaps that's how they all see me.

*Still.*

As an outsider. A city girl who doesn't belong in a small town.

"He's backed off. Plus, he's the one who suggested I stay somewhere else until I can get the window fixed. He seemed genuinely concerned."

"Good." She nods. "Now, has there been any further news about Ryan?"

"No. Nothing yet."

Margaret shakes her head as she makes her way to the doorway. "I'll leave you to settle in. Let me know if you need anything."

"I'm sure I won't. But thanks, Margaret. I'll see you in the morning."

Margaret nods, exits my room, and closes the bedroom door behind her.

———

With the window open, it's tolerable, but still not cool enough for me to fall asleep right away. This house is much smaller than many of the new lakefront homes, a few streets back but a world away. Margaret's part of a sizable group of year-round residents with deep roots in the area, the remnants of what used to be a thriving farming community, and they tend to resent people like me. People who build big, expensive homes on the lakefront and try to dictate its development. I'm certainly not the worst offender, though. At least I live here year-round.

Margaret's home is well kept but time-warped, with all traces of masculinity stripped from the home: pastel tones, flowery bedcovers, lacy linens, as if a man had never lived here. I wonder if that's intentional or if it looked like that when her husband was alive. Perhaps she rid herself of all traces of him to ease her pain and loneliness after his heart attack. She still calls him "my Marty." *Oh, when my Marty was alive, we went to Florida every winter right after Christmas.*

I wonder if Margaret dated at all after her husband's death. Somehow, I doubt it. He died over twenty years ago. She certainly could have remarried by now. Some people never move on, I suppose. Margaret's a retired high school science teacher who was working at the local bookstore when I moved to town. I would pop in and chat with her from time to time.

She still works at the shop one or two days a week. We became acquaintances, not really friends. When Ryan died, Margaret stepped up, unlike the others in this town. Now we seem to fill a void in each other. She reminds me of my grandmother, whose death around the time I met Ryan left me completely alone and dangerously vulnerable.

I think back again to the day I met Ryan. That evening after their classes ended, he took me to a little Mexican restaurant with the best tableside guacamole I'd ever tasted, washed down with tangy margaritas, the perfect amount of salt clinging to our frosty blue glasses.

"So, what's a child life specialist?" he asked.

I explained that a child life specialist is a medical professional who works with sick or injured children, helping them and their families cope with the stress of illnesses, injuries, and disabilities.

He put his hand on mine, a look of reverence in his sparkling aquamarine eyes. "That's incredible. It must take a lot out of you. How do you cope with it?"

I was used to that kind of reaction from men. My choice of profession came with a set of assumptions. I was a caregiver. Tender. Nurturing. Full of self-sacrifice. And when I eventually got knocked off my pedestal, they didn't tend to stick around for very long.

"It's my job," I replied. "I'm capable of compartmentalizing."

I turned the conversation back to him, and he was happy to take the spotlight. He regaled me with stories of his travels around the world as a photojournalist. He'd been all over, to places I'd only read about. Patagonia. Point Barrow, Alaska. Even Antarctica, where he'd endured a two-day journey capped off by a harrowing last leg, bouncing around for hours on a military aircraft with no seats.

My life suddenly seemed small. Provincial. I'd grown up twenty miles from Manhattan and moved to the city for college. Barnard. I'd been there ever since. Sure, I'd back-packed around Europe in college. Did a tour of China and Japan with an old boyfriend. But it had been a safe life devoid of adventure. Predictable. He breathed new life into me, and it was intoxicating. I'd never felt that way about a guy before.

He stopped himself after a few minutes.

"Sorry, Kate. I'm hogging the spotlight."

"It's fine," I replied.

He put his hand on mine and looked into my eyes. "Now tell me. What's the most adventurous thing you've ever done?"

I hesitated. What could I say? Life was something that happened to me, not the other way around. I'd never felt in control of my destiny. Not since my mother died, the first in a series of tragic occurrences in my life. One after the other. Maybe it was time to make things happen.

"Saying yes to you," I replied.

We both smiled, and he leaned over and kissed me.

It was a whirlwind courtship. We made the most of our limited time together. He was on a temporary assignment. One month in Manhattan, assisting with a spread for a travel magazine. We were inseparable, and when he left for his home base in Michigan, I felt as if I were missing a limb. When he showed up in Manhattan the next week and surprised me with a marriage proposal, it felt like something out of a fairytale.

I wasn't expecting it. He flew in and called me from the airport, asking me to meet him at my apartment after work.

I'd given him a key, so he let himself in. When I got home, I barely got in the door when he told me we were going on an adventure. To Central Park, which was a few blocks from my apartment. He'd packed a picnic basket, but he wouldn't let me peek inside.

"No, no," he said when I tried to sneak a look, batting my hand away. "It's a surprise."

I'd never had a man do anything like that for me. It was so romantic that I thought I might burst at the seams. He found a quiet spot on a hilltop where we had a great view but were out of earshot of other parkgoers. Autumn in New York is spectacular, and the trees were ablaze with the colors of fall: crimson, blood orange, mustard yellow, peppered in with various shades of brown and green. The park is a stone's throw from midtown but a world away, where birds chirp, couples stroll, and joggers rack up their mileage. He spread out a blanket and set out a veritable feast. Poached shrimp, couscous with vegetables, chilled chicken breast, and an array of cheeses with table water crackers.

"All my favorites," I said, my eyes wide and my heart full.

"Why are you so surprised? I listen, Kate," Ryan said. "I'm tuned into you."

Then we kissed. A gentle kiss. Tender, not steamy. People were milling about with kids. After we'd gotten through the main course, we fed each other chocolate-covered strawberries, the chocolate slightly melted from the sun's rays. It was a crisp evening but not cold. Perfect sweater weather, but as the sun started to dip behind the tree line, it got a little colder.

"I guess we should head home," I said.

"Not so fast. There's one more course." He smiled, a sly grin that worried me for a moment. I didn't know him all that well, and I was hoping he wasn't suggesting we do something racy in the park. I'm not that kind of girl.

"Stand up," he said, and then he reached into the picnic basket and put his hand behind his back.

I felt perplexed, yet intrigued. Then, to my utter astonishment, he knelt down on one knee, whipped out a ring, and proclaimed his love for me, right smack in the middle of Central Park.

"Kate Sullivan. I fell for you the minute I laid eyes on you. You're the one for me. I love you. Will you marry me?"

His hand shook as he held out the ring, his blue eyes wide and wary. This was a bold move, and I could tell he was nervous about it. That only served to make the moment more endearing. Parkgoers clapped around us, and for a few moments, I stood in front of my kneeling boyfriend, speechless.

I said yes.

*And it was the biggest mistake of my life.*

———

"I'm thinking about selling. After I finish the work on the shoreline revitalization," I say.

I slept a good seven hours, much to my surprise, and awoke relatively refreshed. I'm sipping coffee at the kitchen table, having declined Margaret's offer to make me breakfast. Margret's tinkering around. Putting away the dishes she's already washed and dried. Wiping down the butcher block counters and light wood cabinets, although they appear spotless to me.

"It's a big house for one person," Margaret says. "Maybe

something smaller. Closer to a town center, would be better for you. I know you liked that walking lifestyle in New York."

I realize that Margaret didn't grasp the implication that I'll be leaving the area. I'm not sure when I'll be moving away. It will be, at best, months until I can even put the house on the market. There's no need to upset her by telling her I'm planning to leave town. Not until I have a definite plan.

"I'm getting ahead of myself anyway. I'll need to do the work on the bluff before I put it on the market. And we don't even have an agreement yet about how to fix it."

"Well, with Doug out of the picture, it's sure to go your way. It's a reasonable compromise."

"That's what I thought. But Gavin Mitchell's replacing him."

Margaret's eyes widen. "What? He doesn't even live here."

"That's exactly what I said. He's apparently moved back to be with his mother. The board thinks it's the right thing to do. Letting him stand in for Doug."

"She's a piece of work, that Claudia Mitchell. Always looked down on us, with her family's money. Watch out for that one. Doug was her puppet, you know. She'd send him out to do her dirty work. But that seawall? It was all her idea."

Margaret is a veritable repository of town gossip and history. A very useful person to have on my side. Although I'm not interested in gossip for gossip's sake, it's good to have access to someone who knows where the bodies are buried in this town.

"Good to know," I reply.

"Well, now Gavin will do her bidding. Just watch. She's

got them all wrapped around her little finger. All that family money. She kept control of it, you know."

I do know, but it's good information that it's also common knowledge around town. I wasn't sure about that until now.

"Well, I'm meeting the window guy in thirty minutes," I say.

"Good thing. We're getting some rain today."

"Are we? I didn't see that in the forecast."

"The flies," she says. "I got bitten when I was out in the garden earlier."

I've heard this before from some of the locals. They claim that the flies bite when there's low barometric pressure, indicating an impending storm. "Well then, I need to get going." I grab my overnight bag and head for the front door.

Margaret walks mid-way into the living room and calls out to me with a dishtowel in her hand. "You can stay with me as long as you like, Kate. If you're uncomfortable alone."

"Oh, no. I'll be fine once the window's fixed. I'm going to install an alarm, too. And better cameras. But thanks, Margaret. For everything."

"Sure. You take care, dear. And watch your back. The puppet master will probably have it in for you now."

My eyes pop open. "Wait. What? You think that Claudia may have . . ."

Margaret puts her hands on her hips. "I think Claudia may have what, Kate?"

I let out a breath I'd been holding. "Oh. You mean she'll come after me about the bluff."

"Of course. What did you think I was implying? That Claudia Mitchell killed her own husband?"

"No. Not at all. That would be . . . ridiculous." I throw up my hands, and a nervous chuckle slips out. "I mean, why would she kill her own husband?"

"Only three reasons I can think of that a wife kills her husband. Money? No. Claudia had control of it. Self-defense? I suppose she could have been a battered wife and kept it from everyone. You never know what's happening behind closed doors. But I doubt it."

She pauses, her head cocked to one side, looking curiously at me.

"And the third reason?" I ask.

"An affair," Margaret says, nodding. "The green monster."

I swallow and look away. "Right. I suppose an affair would do it." I take a breath. "Well, I need to get a move on. Thanks again, Margaret."

She smiles. "Good luck with the window, Kate." Dish-towel in hand, she waves me off.

My chest tightens, and I slip out her door without another word.

# CHAPTER 6
## TRAVIS

'll be damned," Travis says as he takes in the crime scene.

"You can say that again." Sloane reaches into her purse, pulls out her phone, and snaps a photo as they approach Doug Mitchell's vessel, sandwiched between rows of various-sized boats and yachts, hiding in plain sight.

A Coast Guard officer introduces himself and proceeds to give them the rundown. Doug Mitchell's Sundancer sat for three days in a slip, rocking gently to the rhythm of the currents, safely moored at a dock a few towns away. When the slip's proper tenant returned to Saugatuck after a few nights away and tried to dock his boat, he called in, reportedly outraged that some idiot had parked in his spot.

*A dead idiot.*

His tune reportedly changed when he was informed of this, along with the fact that he'd need to stay and answer a few questions after they found an alternate place for him to dock. The officer did a cursory interview, and the man swore he'd never heard of Doug Mitchell. He was away on a trip to

Canada, visiting friends who could verify his story. The man was instructed not to leave town. He was informed that the Sundancer was now a crime scene, so the vessel would need to stay put until the investigation was concluded. By the time Travis and Sloane arrived on the scene, the slip's owner had already left.

Travis takes in the sight of the cruiser. The cause and manner of death are still under investigation. Even putting a rush on it, the results normally take a week or so to come in. If someone docked the boat, then it seems clear to him that it was a homicide. And since it likely happened out on the lake, Coast Guard Investigative Services, or C-GIS, technically has jurisdiction. They've already taken control of the crime scene. They're based in Detroit, though, which could really slow things down.

"Can we have a look?" Travis asks the officer. "We think this death might be related to another case of ours."

Maritime jurisdiction is complicated, and Travis wonders if the killer planned it that way. Killing Ryan Breslow on land and Doug Mitchell at sea is a great way to slow down an investigation. He explains his theory to the officer, and Sloane plays along, although he's stretching the truth a bit, trying to frame it as part of an ongoing investigation. Normally, the Coast Guard isn't very territorial, and he's hoping this is one of those times.

"We can work with you, but it's up to C-GIS to officially release the case. You'll need to loop in Detroit."

"Got it. Thanks."

They don their gloves and booties, sign in, and prepare to inspect the vessel. The two of them board and start to poke around. A cooler sits next to a deck chair. Inside it are two unopened water bottles. No half-empty bottles or glasses are to be found anywhere. No sign of a scuffle. No blood, although that could have been cleaned up. The forensics team is on its way, so they'll know about that soon enough.

"Seems odd that he would be out here on the lake, drinking . . . nothing," Sloane says.

"I was thinking the same thing."

Claudia Mitchell said that her husband liked to go out on the lake and sip a cocktail to unwind. Even if he wasn't likely to imbibe before a big meeting, it seems that he would drink *something*. Water. Iced tea. The absence of an empty cup or water bottle is conspicuous.

"Maybe down below?" she says.

Travis nods.

They head down the narrow stairway, Sloane first, both crouching to avoid hitting their heads in the cramped space. It makes him a little claustrophobic, these tiny cabins. He's never understood the appeal.

They inspect the living area, which consists of a built-in cabinet and bar area, a small sectional seating area that converts to a bed, and a small closet. They check the surfaces and garbage cans. No beverage containers.

"I'll take the bathroom?" Travis says. "You stay in here?"

"It's called the head," Sloane replies.

He rolls his eyes. Sloane's a water woman. Him, not so much. They go about their respective tasks. Travis combs meticulously through the miniature medicine cabinet.

Dramamine.

Toothbrush and toothpaste.

Mouthwash.

*Someone sure wants to have fresh breath.*

He makes a mental note to ask Claudia Mitchell if anyone in the family is prone to seasickness. Other than that, there's not much else of note. At least that he can see with the naked eye.

"Travis!" Sloane calls out.

Travis rushes into the living area. He's not too shocked to see a lacy red thong dangling from the large tweezers she holds in her hand. This had all the trappings of an affair, even before he found the mouthwash. Claudia Mitchell's not stupid, either. Did she believe her husband's clear-my-head-on-the-boat excuses? He doubts it.

"Where'd you find that?" he asks.

"It was stuffed underneath the cushions."

"So, what do you think?" he asks.

"I think Doug Mitchell's been a naughty boy." Sloane photographs and bags the evidence.

"What? You can't see Claudia Mitchell rocking a red thong? Maybe it's their thing. Stow away on the boat. Spice things up a bit." He smirks.

"I guess you never can tell with people. But if these aren't hers, we've got a motive."

As they're finishing up their preliminary search of the vessel, the forensics team arrives. It's a cramped crime scene, so Travis and Sloane disembark and turn it over to them, prepared to wait patiently for some news.

A call comes across his cell. It's the precinct. A neighbor caught footage of the person who threw the brick through Kate Breslow's window.

"You go," Sloane says. "I'll stay here until they're finished. I'll meet you back at the office."

———

Travis plays the video again. The image is clear for security camera video. The perpetrator's hoodie blocks the person's face while she's on Kate's property. But as she retreats to the neighbor's yard, she gets careless. The hoodie falls from her head, exposing her face to their camera. She pulls the hoodie back up, but not in time.

Kate Breslow has already identified the woman from the text Travis sent. It's a friend of her late husband's, she claims. Travis asked Breslow to come in and view it in person. Make a statement.

"It's her," Breslow confirms after looking at it twice. "I'm sure of it."

The perp's an environmentalist by the name of Daisy Parker. A pale, thin woman in her early thirties with mousy brown hair and small, beady eyes, according to Kate Breslow. Travis finds Kate Breslow's description a bit harsh. He's already pulled up some social media photos of the woman. She's not a raving beauty, but she's attractive in an earthy kind of way.

"And what was your husband's relationship with this woman?"

"She was an associate of his," Breslow replies.

"In your text, you said Daisy Parker was a friend of your husband's. Which is it? Friend or associate?"

"I'm not sure. Does it really matter?"

"Your husband was killed in a suspicious manner, and now you've been threatened. Yes, it matters. Why didn't you tell me about her earlier?"

She sits up on her haunches now, like she's about to bolt. "There was nothing to tell. You asked me if I had any enemies. She's not my enemy. I told you everything I knew about the threats. I told you I felt Ryan was in deeper with some of the environmental groups than he let on. And I turned over his computer to you over a year ago."

Travis has that feeling again. The same pang in the gut he had when he was investigating Ryan Breslow's death the first time. Kate Breslow's hiding something. There's more to this than meets the eye. She doesn't seem like a murderer to him, though.

"Do you have any idea why this woman would have it in for you?" he asks.

Her brow furrows. "What are you getting at?"

"I'm not getting at anything. I'm merely trying to find out why this woman threw a brick through your window. I have to say, though, the fact that you're getting so defensive?" Travis shakes his head. "It makes me wonder if there isn't something more going on."

"I'm assuming it's because she doesn't like my plan for the shoreline," she says.

Travis smirks. "We're bringing her in soon, so I guess we'll find out."

"Well, good. If there are no more questions, I'd like to get going."

"Sure thing, Ms. Breslow. We'll be in touch."

She stands up, brushes herself off, and heads for the door.

"Don't forget to look into that alarm," Travis calls out to her.

"Thanks for the reminder," she says.

What is it about this woman that bothers him so much? Is it the fact that she didn't present like a grieving widow when her husband died? Over the years, he's learned that some people are like that. They hold back in front of strangers. There's a melancholy air about her that doesn't smack of black widow, but he can't decide if she's simply stoic or consumed with guilt. Perhaps she ran her husband off the road in the heat of the moment, angry or hurt about something, and then regretted it immediately. A momentary lapse of judgment.

*And there's only one thing he can think of that would make a woman snap like that.*

———

Daisy Parker is a waif of a woman. And Travis has to admit, in person, the woman's eyes are a little beady. She's got a wounded bird look about her. She's dressed in jeans and a light brown sweater that hangs off her thin frame. Most people feel nervous inside an interrogation room. The locked door. The bright lights. But she appears unfazed, even confident.

*At least on the surface.*

Daisy is a nickname. Frances Parker is her real name. She lives in Chikaming, a few towns away. She works at a coffee shop and freelances as a journalist, mostly for environmental websites and magazines. She claims that's how she met Ryan Breslow. She interviewed him for an article she was writing, and he let her use some of his photographs for it, free of charge.

Travis fears that it will be a short meeting. She's denied that it was her on the video and seems ready to pack it in. Leave the burden of proof to them. Travis tried the good cop routine. Acted like he was on her side. Pretended to share her ire about the shoreline situation. And he's gotten nowhere.

Sloane pokes her head in and calls him out of the interrogation room. He leaves Daisy to stew for a bit as they huddle in the doorway. Then he strolls back over, plops down across from her, steeples his hands, and looks her in the eye.

"Doug Mitchell's death's been ruled a homicide."

She sits up straighter. "What? Wait. I had nothing to do with that."

"I didn't say that you did. Why would you make that assumption?"

She swallows and takes a moment to regroup, looking off to the side as she fiddles with a long, thin strand of hair, the same color as her oversized sweater.

"Okay. What do you want to know?" She leans in now, looking a bit like a schoolgirl in the principal's office, eager to throw a classmate under the bus and save herself.

"I want you to tell me about your relationship with Ryan Breslow," Travis says.

"I already told you. He was an associate of mine."

"His wife described you as a friend."

Daisy rolls her eyes. "Get me an attorney. One of those public defenders. Then I'll tell you everything I know. But I had nothing to do with Doug Mitchell's death."

"Fair enough," Travis says. "We might be here a while. Care for a beverage?"

"I'm a camel," she says. "I'm very patient, too, so don't worry about me." She folds her arms and leans back in the chair with a smug smirk on her face.

*Worth a try.*

Either she's been coached by some activist organization, or this isn't her first run-in with the law. He excuses himself to comply with her request. But as he reaches the doorway, he turns around for one more look. Her face has turned a shade paler, and the smug look is gone. She's got something to tell him.

*And she's nervous about it.*

# CHAPTER 7
## KATE

he gaping hole from last night has been replaced by a shiny new sheet of glass, and my hardwood floors are pristine and free of debris. But an uncomfortable silence settles over the living room, and the sound of shattering glass rings in my memory like a warning bell. I want desperately to leave this place behind.

*Now, more than ever.*

The alarm company can't get anyone over until later in the week. Although I'm relieved that they caught Daisy Parker, I'm still on edge. The meeting with Travis Whittaker didn't help. So much for laying off me. What happened to change his attitude? He was almost human to me last night. I'm afraid for my life, and he doesn't seem to understand that. Someone may have killed Doug, and they very well could be after me.

I look around and take a rare moment to feel proud of what I've accomplished. When Ryan talked me into coming with him to Crest Lake, he sold it as a short-term proposition. He'd bought this fixer-upper years before we met, and the idea was to renovate the home, sell it, and move on, securing financial freedom and the ability to do whatever we wanted from there.

A fixer-upper was an understatement. It was barely a cottage when we arrived, and that should have been my first clue that he was full of shit. Back then, I was in that all-consuming, life-affirming place in a relationship where the heart rules over the head. Our bed was a sanctuary. A hideaway from the world. A place where we sometimes stayed for days on end. Making love. Baring our souls. Stopping briefly to eat food we'd ordered or sometimes forgetting to eat at all.

*Pure infatuation.*

*The kind that blinds you to reality.*

Not love, although that's what it felt like at the time. A dopamine and oxytocin-induced euphoria. I've been studying this over the last few years as part of my research for a doctorate in clinical psychology. And to make sure I never make the same mistake again.

Ryan's not stupid. He made me think it was my idea to go in on the renovation. It was my inheritance that financed it. I can see now that it was part of his plan to control me.

*Completely.*

The home is unrecognizable now from that tiny cottage, which was repurposed as a guest suite. It's worth a small fortune by Michigan's standards because of the location. Not overly large or ostentatious, but classic. Four bedrooms. Three bathrooms. Craftsman style. Solidly built with natural materials that blend with the scenery and make the most of the stunning lakefront view.

But we hadn't expected so much erosion to happen in such a short time. Over a period of five years, we've lost twenty feet of property. Twenty feet of bluff. A bluff that sits eighty feet above the shoreline, with my home inching ever closer to the edge. If I can push my plan through and secure the home for a few more decades, I can still cash out with a substantial profit. I need to try. It was my life savings, and I need to recover it in order to move on before it's no longer an option. One bad storm season could ruin me if we don't do something, and there's nothing holding me here anymore.

But what about Whittaker? How much does he know? What does he suspect? I wonder what Daisy Parker will tell him. I'm pretty sure that whatever it is, it won't be good for either of us. Hopefully, it will deflect his attention away from me, at least for a while. Buy me some time to figure a way out of this mess.

*And that's better than nothing.*

———

"Hello?" Margaret calls to me through the screen door. "Kate? Are you home?"

Although I'm not in the mood for company, I appreciate Margaret's support, so I put on a happy face and answer the door.

Margaret's made a lasagna for me. "I don't need to come in," she says. "I wanted to drop this off. Figured you'd be too busy to cook."

I unlock the screen door and invite her in, knowing that she probably doesn't have much else going on today. It's just after lunchtime, and Margaret likes her afternoon tea.

I offer, and Margaret accepts, following me into the kitchen with her tray of lasagna. I put on the water for her tea, and Margaret sits on a stool at my island counter, resting her elbows on the dark granite surface. It's a chef's kitchen with a large farmhouse sink, a Forno gas range, and a convection oven—totally wasted on me, but great for resale purposes.

"Earl Grey?" I ask.

Margaret nods. "Maybe it's none of my business, Kate. But you may want to replace that keypad lock on the front door. If someone's casing your place, they could see you punch in the code. Then they'd be able to get inside."

"Good point, Margaret. I never thought about that."

"Any news about your window? Looks like new."

"In fact, there is. I was able to identify the woman from the video footage at my neighbor's house."

Her brows rise. "It was a woman?"

"Yes. Daisy Parker's her name. She was an associate of Ryan's."

Margaret looks curiously at me, visibly intrigued. "What kind of associate?"

I sigh. "She's an activist. One of the more radical ones."

"One of the crazies, you mean?" Margaret rolls her eyes. "Good lord."

"Yes," I say. "They're very riled up about the shoreline."

"Silly girl. Throwing a brick through a window. Not a very sophisticated move."

I place a mug of tea in front of Margaret and take a seat across from her.

Margaret blows on her tea and then takes a cautious sip. "You need some proper teacups, Kate. Who drinks tea from a coffee mug?"

I shrug, and she shakes her head.

"Why would Ryan get mixed up with a girl like that?" she asks.

Margaret's not stupid, and I sense that she's fishing here,

but I'm not giving anything up. The last thing I need is the gossip mill churning about my marriage. She's a nice lady, and she means well, but she likes to gab with everyone.

"I'm not sure they were mixed up, per se," I reply. "But as I said, Ryan had drifted more into their camp over the years."

She nods. "Well, at least you can relax a bit. They caught her. She can't harm you now."

*She can, though.*

It puts my stomach in knots as I think about what Daisy Parker may have told the detectives. I can only hope that the woman is not as dumb as she seems because telling them everything wouldn't be good.

*For either of us.*

# CHAPTER 8
## TRAVIS

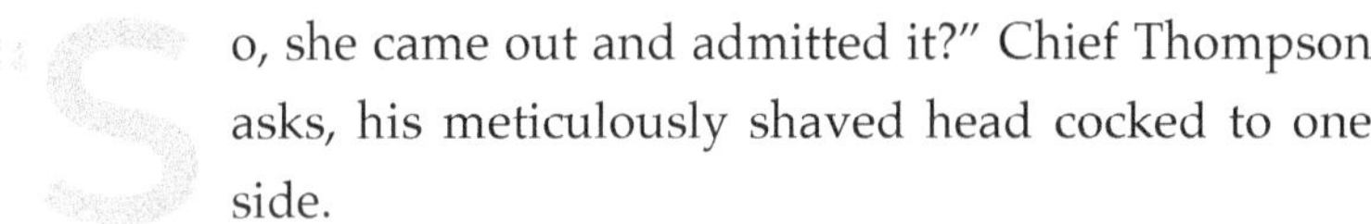

"So, she came out and admitted it?" Chief Thompson asks, his meticulously shaved head cocked to one side.

"Yes," Travis replies.

The police chief is a formidable man with a thick neck and broad shoulders. The sleeves of his uniform strain to contain his massive biceps as he pages through the paperwork Travis handed to him a few minutes earlier.

"She claims it started about two years before he died," Sloane adds.

Sloane is referring to the revelation that Daisy Parker was having an affair with Ryan Breslow. Well, not simply an affair. The woman claims that, at the time of Breslow's death, they were in love. And that the Breslow marriage was in trouble.

"So, she threw the brick through the window to intimidate Kate Breslow? Get her to back off on her proposal?" Chief Thompson asks.

"Yes," Travis replies. "That's what she claims. To 'protect

Ryan's legacy' is how she put it. She swears she's not after Kate Breslow. She wanted her to back off her proposal."

Thompson sits with this information for a bit, his lips pursed.

Doug Mitchell's official cause of death was drowning, they now know, but he had some kind of sedative in his system; the tox screen will take more time. Their best guess is that someone crushed up the drug, put it in his drink, and then pushed him overboard when he was incapacitated. Someone sanitized the crime scene and docked the boat, so they knew it wasn't an accident. Travis has his suspicions about the red panties they found under the cushions. It seems a bit too convenient. Perhaps someone is being framed.

Travis has already started to spin this information in a variety of ways. He senses that Chief Thompson is doing the same. Not only does an affair give Kate Breslow a motive to kill her husband, but it also gives Daisy Parker a reason to want to see Kate squirm if, in fact, there was an affair.

Parker could be lying, too. Trying to deflect their attention from whatever their radical organization is up to. Although Daisy swore up and down she had nothing to do with Doug Mitchell's death, he's not ruling her out.

"She agreed to give you a DNA sample as part of the deal?" Thompson asks.

"Yes. She agreed to tell us what she knew about Ryan Breslow and pay a fine if we dropped the charge to vandalism," Sloane says. "And she's already supplied her DNA. She says she had nothing to do with Mitchell's death, and she wants to be ruled out."

"You're going to pay Kate Breslow a visit, I take it?" Thompson says.

"Yes. We wanted to brief you first," Travis says.

"Good. Go over there. Shake her up a little. See what falls out. She had to know. Wives always know. The question is, why did she keep it from us?" Thompson says.

"Right. Will do, Chief," Sloane replies. "Travis was planning to head over there. I'm going to the lab to see if they can put a rush on the DNA analysis."

Thompson nods, and they head out of his office.

————

Travis raps on the screen door, a bit surprised that the window's been fixed already. After a few moments, Kate Breslow comes to the door.

"What can I do for you?" she asks.

"I wanted to fill you in on the investigation," Travis says.

"I, um. I have company," Breslow says. "It's not a great time."

"It'll only take a minute. It's important."

After a few minutes of stalling, she invites him in.

A voice calls out from across the room.

"If it isn't Travis Whittaker! My star student."

*Margaret Brenner.*

*Great.*

"Well, hello there, Margaret," Travis replies.

Margaret makes her way over to them.

"Always a pleasure." He hadn't realized that the two of them were more than acquaintances.

"I wanted to come over and check on Kate. It's terrible. Those radicals are out to ruin this town. Have you found out anything more?" Margaret asks.

"I can't comment on an ongoing investigation."

"Of course," Margaret says. She eyes them for a few

awkward moments and finally seems to get the drift. "Well, I suppose I should be going. Let the two of you get down to business."

"That would be best, Margaret," Travis says.

Kate sees Margaret out the door, and Travis takes a few moments to look around the house. It looks as if nothing happened here last night.

*She's good at cleaning up messes.*

Soon, Kate stands in front of him, her arms crossed with a defiant look on her face. If she's intimidated by his visit, she's not showing it.

"What did you want to tell me?" she asks.

"Let's sit," he says, motioning to the sofa. "This might be difficult to hear."

"I'd prefer to make this quick," she replies.

"Okay then, I'll get right to it. Daisy Parker claims she was having an affair with your husband."

Her face goes a shade paler, indicating fear but not surprise.

"She claims they were in love. And that your marriage was in trouble."

"Why are you telling me this?" Breslow asks.

"I thought you'd want to know. But from the look on your face, I'm guessing this isn't new information."

She looks off to the side.

"Did you know about your husband's affair?"

"Am I under arrest?" she asks.

"No," Travis replies.

"Then I need to ask you to please leave my house. If you have any more questions, you can talk to my attorney." Her voice is polite, and her mannerisms courteous, but she may as well have told him to fuck off.

Travis smirks. "Sure," he says. "If that's how you want to play it."

She opens the front door for him. "Please, Detective Whittaker. Go. And try to do your job. Find my husband's killer. And Doug's. Before someone else gets hurt. As I see it, I'm probably next on the list."

It's a smart move. Even if she had nothing to do with her husband's death, if she knew about the affair, she withheld it when they were investigating last year. That's a problem for her.

As he walks to his car, Travis grabs his phone to call Sloane, anxious to see if she found out anything more about the DNA and the origin of the red panties they found on the boat. Because if Ryan Breslow was having an affair with Daisy Parker, he can't help but think that sleeping with Doug Mitchell would be the ultimate payback.

# CHAPTER 9
## KATE

shut the front door, close the drapes, and collapse on the sofa. I've never felt so alone. And given my background, that's saying something. My hands start to shake, and I feel as if I might cry. I lean into it, thinking of all the sad things in my life, trying to make it come. If I could cry, that would mean progress for me.

But the metal gates come crashing down in front of the memories, shielding me from the pain, leaving only images but no emotion, as if I'm remembering a movie I saw rather than my own life. It's a terrible feeling, like when you almost sneeze, but then you don't. And now it's stuck in there, needling you.

*I'm broken.*

*And broken people don't cry.*

It was a little over four years into our marriage when Ryan and I were invited over to the Mitchell's home for dinner. It was an early spring evening. Our renovation was almost finished, but it was clear that Ryan didn't want to make good on his promise to cash out and leave Crest Lake. In this town, he was a big fish in a small pond, unlike back in New York, and he relished the spotlight. The activists fed his ego, using his photographs to help advance their cause. His work, I must admit, is quite excellent, and he had compiled a repository of images chronicling the deterioration of the shoreline in Crest Lake and other towns on Lake Michigan.

Meanwhile, a series of high-water years had dramatically impacted our property. The Mitchells constructed a seawall in front of their home, which hastened the erosion for the rest of us. Talks about the crumbling bluff had started, and they became more urgent after the southern stairs collapsed a month later, killing a tourist. I wanted to protect my investment and help make the area safer. So, I got myself on the committee that was overseeing the shoreline revitalization proposals for the town and soon became the chair.

Doug Mitchell was on the town council board and, like me, had a vested interest in the fate of the shoreline. He was also on the committee, but we had yet to meet as a group. I figured the dinner invitation was a way to find some common ground on our approach to the bluff. We'd met in passing, but didn't know each other very well.

Ryan wore jeans and a brown sweater, and he sulked like a teenager on the walk over. One of his go-to moves to bend me to his will. He and the Mitchells were already at odds over the issue of the bluff, and I had been formulating a compromise. Ryan's hold on me was waning, but I didn't let on about that. I was planning to make the most of the evening, regardless of how he felt. I'd done some research and was hoping to have an intelligent conversation about it.

I wore an emerald green sleeveless dress that hugged my body and accented my pale green eyes, making them appear a bit richer in hue. Claudia greeted us at the door, looking classy and elegant in black slacks that flattered her figure and a modest white blouse with a ruffle down the front. She looked me up and down. I hadn't given much consideration to my neckline, but maybe I should have. It wasn't exactly plunging, but it was more revealing than Claudia's, and I suddenly felt a bit too exposed.

Doug Mitchell didn't seem to notice, though. He kept his gaze at eye level. Dressed in slacks and a navy sweater, he invited us in and offered me his hand. His grip was warm and dry. Formidable. Like a powerful CEO hosting a board meeting. Then he sandwiched my hand with his free one and gave it a little squeeze as he welcomed me into his home. It felt reassuring. He did the same thing to Ryan. Next to him, my husband seemed like a man-child. And he acted like one, too.

The evening started out cordially. The requisite pleasantries were exchanged. I gave Claudia the bean dip I made, which she reluctantly placed on the coffee table. We sat in the living room. Their home is formal and stately with dark, heavy drapes, wainscoted walls, and a collection of valuable antiques elegantly peppered in with the regal furnishings. Not the kind of home that invites levity. There was tension in the air from the start, although everyone was still on their best behavior in the beginning.

"You shouldn't have," she said.

*She meant it, too.*

Doug offered us a glass of Pinot Noir, a 2021 Aubert from Sonoma. He didn't brag about it, but I know wine, and that one is on the pricey side. He mesmerized me right from the start. The way he talked with his hands seemed to perfectly accent what he was saying. I couldn't stop looking at them. They were powerful and commanding. I thought about what those hands would feel like, sliding across my thigh—a thought that caught me totally off guard. He ate my bean dip, too, although it wasn't a great pairing with the wine. Not to mention, the seasoning was a bit off. He ate it, though, which is more than I can say for everyone else.

After twenty minutes or so, Claudia informed us that it was time to be seated for dinner. We stood. Doug put his hand on the small of my back, directing me to the dining room, and a delightful tingle rippled through my body. His hand placement wasn't lost on Claudia, who shot me a look, her nostrils flaring ever so slightly.

Ryan was oblivious. He'd been sleeping with other women for years and had long since lost interest in me. Daisy Parker was one of many, and I can't help but feel a bit sorry for her, confessing to the detectives about their undying love as if they were somehow meant to be. The only person Ryan Breslow loved was himself, and maybe someday, I'll tell her so.

As soon as the salads were served, my man-child husband started in. He set down his fork, leaned back in his high-backed rosewood chair, and crossed his arms.

"So, let's put this all on the table. Why are we really here?" Ryan asked.

I found his behavior embarrassing. Catching Doug's eye, I offered him an apologetic shrug.

"Ryan. We're on the same team here," Doug offered. "We're neighbors. We want the same thing. To protect our property and the shoreline."

Doug was cool. Collected. Like someone trying to talk down a mental patient on the verge of a breakdown. He spoke in a soothing voice that bordered on condescending and that only served to egg Ryan on.

Ryan went on the offensive, his eyes filled with scorn. He leaned over towards Doug, who was sitting at the head of the table. "Your seawall made the problem worse." He slammed his palm down on the tabletop. "Now you want to extend it? Are you kidding me? How many more people have to die before you realize that some things are bigger than you?"

"Ryan!" I implored. "Let's not do this, okay? We're here to talk. And I've been doing some research. I have some ideas."

"Oh, you have some ideas, do you, Kate? Why don't you tell us about them if you're such an expert all of a sudden?"

The Mitchells turned to each other, seemingly uncomfortable with being thrust into the middle of our marital spat. Ryan caught himself and took a breath. His face softened, and he reached his hand across the table to me.

"Sorry, Kate. The wine must be going to my head. I've been researching this for decades now. It's kinda my thing, you know?"

An awkward silence filled the air, and then things settled down. We started nibbling on our first course. My blood boiled, but I contained my anger, reducing it to a slow simmer. I had a plan to end my marriage and move on, and that plan involved playing dumb. Letting Ryan think he was getting away with his outrageous behavior—until it was time to strike.

This was new, though. He'd never lashed out at me in public. He seemed to be escalating, and I realized I had to move faster.

I went on to explain my idea of reangling the bluff and constructing a revetment. Doug gave me his full attention. He asked me intelligent questions, and I answered them. Then it was Claudia's turn to explode.

"You have the space for it, Kate. We don't!" Claudia said.

It was true. If we went through with my plan, it would be worse for the Mitchells than for us. Their house was closer to the edge than all the others. They would need to move their house back because reangling the bluff would take up another chunk of their property, and they'd be in violation of the setback law.

"I know you'd have to move your house back. But that's not the end of the world. You have the space."

They own the lot behind their house, as well as several others that had yet to be developed, so this wasn't fatal for them. But any way you sliced it, they'd lose property value.

"That would reduce the size of the lot behind our house, and you know it," Claudia said. "We're about to break ground. We'd have to redo the plans. Reduce the size of the structure we're building on that lot to conform with the zoning laws."

I tried to mollify her. "Claudia. This isn't anyone's fault. We all need to make sacrifices. In the long run—"

"In the long run?" she said. "You've been here all of five years. I've spent my whole life in this town. There have been decades when the water's receded. It will again. Everyone's overreacting. All this hysteria about climate change. The climate has always changed, Kate!" Claudia shot her husband a look, obviously pissed off that he wasn't backing her up.

Doug came to her rescue. "Yes, Kate. My wife's right about this, in terms of the history of the lake over the last few decades. I've compiled the data. And I plan to bring it to our first meeting next week. But Claudia? I'd like to hear Ryan out on this if that's okay. He's done a lot of work in the neighboring townships, and I'd like to know what he thinks."

Doug gave his wife a knowing look, one that said *I've got this. Trust me.*

Claudia took a deep breath. "Sure. Why don't you tell us what you've found, Ryan?" She gave her husband a subtle nod. They were a team now, it seemed to me, although Ryan didn't pick up on it. He'd turned around to grab his phone from his jacket pocket.

It was a brilliant strategy, playing to Ryan's ego. He took the spotlight and filled them in on all he had uncovered. He pulled up some of his photographs on his phone and showed them off. As I said, his photography is excellent, and they were rightly impressed. Soon, the subject changed to Ryan's adventures around the world, and he captivated them as he'd once dazzled me.

I figured it was a tactic. Doug Mitchell simply wanted to know what the environmentalists were thinking so he could counter them. It worked like a charm. We got through the rest of the meal without further incident. I even had a chance to talk about myself a little, which hardly ever happened, being married to a man like my husband.

Claudia was in the kitchen, and Ryan had gone to the bathroom. Doug asked me what I did back in New York. I told him I was a child life specialist at a major children's hospital in Manhattan and explained briefly about what that entailed. It's not a high-paying profession, I informed him, but at least in a large metropolis like New York, there were full-time jobs in my profession with benefits. I was pretty set financially back then, with no mortgage and ample savings, so I could afford to take a lower-paying job. In Crest Lake, though, with the nearest children's hospital over an hour away, my practice had effectively deteriorated. Once in a while, I'd be called in on a contract basis, but it wasn't enough to live on, so I needed a new plan.

"I've been working on a doctorate in clinical psychology,

which pays much better than a child life specialist position. I've also been focusing on our home renovation," I explained. "And now, I'll be working on the shoreline revitalization proposal."

"Seems a shame to give up on such a laudable profession," he said.

Then our spouses came back, interrupting our intimate moment. The four of us shared a nightcap. Claudia appeared to be placated by the little interlude between her and her husband when they teamed up to calm Ryan. Doug had her back, it seemed to me, and he was gathering ammunition to go after what she wanted.

*Or so I thought.*

But Doug Mitchell had already made up his mind to back my plan. Because that evening, although I didn't know it yet, he'd already fallen head over heels in love with me.

We finished our nightcap and headed out. On the walk back, Ryan's civil façade crumbled. "Don't ever contradict me like that in front of people again, Kate. And get off that damn committee."

*Or what, Ryan?*

*What're you going to do?*

I didn't talk back to him that night. As I said, I had a plan.

*And Ryan would never see it coming.*

But now Ryan is dead, and so is Doug Mitchell. I should call my attorney, but frankly, I can't afford him. My marriage to Ryan and the home renovation used up most of my inheritance, and I spent the life insurance proceeds on attorney's fees last year when I was a person of interest in Ryan's accident. What remains of my inheritance will need to go towards the work on the shoreline revitalization expenses.

Maybe Whittaker's visit was simply a fishing expedition.

Nothing has come of Ryan's hit and run, and I had nothing to do with Doug's death. They can't possibly have any evidence against me for that. But then, I have no real alibi for the time Doug was out on the boat. I was home.

*Alone.*

Getting ready for the council meeting.

Rather than catastrophize, I tell myself to take a deep breath and try to focus on something I can control. Getting my plan approved, fixing the bluff, and cashing out. I didn't kill Doug, but I know how this will look if Whittaker finds out I was sleeping with him. And with Gavin Mitchell taking Doug's seat, he'll back his mother's plan.

I need to secure another board member, get the plan approved, and cash out.

*And I need to do it fast.*

# CHAPTER 10
## TRAVIS

Travis hears the clicking of Sloane's spike heels on the tile floor. Although his back is to the door, he knows it's her because most other women around here wear flats. He turns around to see her charging into the precinct's bullpen with a vengeance, waving the DNA results in her hand, talking a mile a minute.

"Wait. What did you say?" Travis cocks his head to one side, thinking he must have misunderstood her.

"I said the DNA on the red thong belongs to Daisy Parker," Sloane repeats.

"Daisy Parker?" His eyes nearly pop out of his head.

"Yep." She hands him the results. Her dark brown Coach handbag lands on the table with a thud. She doesn't sit yet.

He's flabbergasted. "You're telling me that Doug Mitchell was having an affair with Daisy Parker?"

"No. I'm telling you that Daisy Parker's DNA was on the thong we found on his boat." Sloane says.

She hands the results to Travis, sits across from him, and opens up the case folder in the center of the conference table.

He sits with the information for a bit, scratching his head, staring at the results, which he finds hard to believe.

Travis catches her up on his meeting with Kate Breslow, and they both agree that she probably knew about her husband's affair. Then they settle into a period of silent reflection, both of them trying to make sense of this new information.

"So, what do you make of it?" Travis asks. "Think it's a set-up? I had my suspicions even before this happened."

"Probably. I can't see Doug Mitchell hooking up with Feral Cheryl."

"Who the hell is Feral Cheryl?"

Sloane rolls her eyes. "She was this hippy doll from Australia I had when I was a kid. I wanted a Barbie, but my mother's a diehard feminist. Feral Cheryl was supposed to be a compromise, but she was more like the anti-Barbie. Barefoot. Tattooed. Carried around a bag of herbs. Probably a vegetarian. Definitely an environmentalist."

Travis takes in Sloane's outfit: classic navy pantsuit, perfectly styled hair, and a string of pearls around her neck.

"I assume this backfired on your mother," Travis says.

She shrugs. "Usually does."

"Well, set-up or not, we need to pay Claudia Mitchell a visit. It'll be interesting to gauge her reaction," Travis says.

"I know. I hate to sound salacious, but it is intriguing. Daisy Parker's panties are found on Doug Mitchell's boat, but then she claims she was in love with Ryan Breslow. What's next?"

"Yeah. It's like Peyton Place around here," Travis replies.

"What's Peyton's Place?" Sloane asks.

"*Peyton* Place. It was a show my grandmother used to . . ."

He shakes his head. "You know? Never mind. Let's go. We've got a homicide to solve."

———

"Mrs. Mitchell, we've got some news for you," Sloane says from the stoop outside the front door. "It might be difficult to hear."

"Please call me Claudia, Sloane. I've known you for years."

Sloane's jaw stiffens. "This is a formal visit," she says. "I'm here in an official capacity. But if it makes you more comfortable, I'm happy to comply with your request. *Claudia.*" Her eyes widen as she holds Claudia Mitchell in her gaze.

"Come in," Claudia says, waving them through the door, seemingly oblivious to the fact that she's pissed off Sloane.

Travis and Sloane follow her to the living room. It's not lost on Travis that Claudia Mitchell didn't extend the same courtesy to them, addressing them by their formal titles. She went with first names, and that kind of thing bugs Sloane. She's a stickler for formalities. The two of them decided beforehand that Sloane should be the one to break the news, woman to woman. It seemed better that way, but now Travis is having second thoughts.

"Please. Have a seat." Claudia motions to the brown leather sofa, then sits across from them in a cream wingback chair with subtle white stripes. The two of them sit on the sofa. "What have you come to tell me, Sloane?" Claudia asks.

"We've obtained DNA evidence from the Sundancer, belonging to a person of interest," Sloane says.

"That's wonderful news." Claudia's eyes widen. "Whose is it? Are you making an arrest?"

Sloane glances at Travis, and he takes over. "The DNA belongs to a woman named Daisy Parker," Travis says. "She's an environmentalist from Chikaming. The same person who threw a brick through Kate Breslow's window a few nights ago."

"Oh, my god. Do you think those radical ecoterrorists killed my husband? I knew they were dangerous, but nobody would listen to me."

"We're not at liberty to discuss the case, and no arrests have been made in your husband's death," Sloane says. "I can tell you that Daisy Parker confessed to throwing the brick. And with her DNA being found on the boat. Well, you see how it looks. But she swears she had nothing to do with your husband's death."

"And you believe her? Why would you believe her?" Claudia's voice shoots up an octave.

Travis jumps in. "Sloane didn't say that we believe the woman. But we're getting ahead of ourselves. We want to show you a photo. See if you recognize her. Maybe you can help us. Place her in the vicinity or something."

"Of course," Claudia says.

Travis pulls out his phone and scrolls through a few photos of Daisy Parker. Claudia studies them carefully, then leans back in her chair and crosses her legs.

"No." She shakes her head. "I've never seen this woman before," Claudia says, with no flash of recognition in her eyes and not a hint of hesitation.

Travis believes her.

"I need to ask you a question, Claudia, and it's not an easy thing to ask," he says.

"Go ahead, Travis," Claudia says.

"Was your husband having an affair?"

Her shoulders tense up, and it's obvious he's struck a nerve. She looks away, her lips pressed, as she fiddles with the edge of her cardigan. Then she sits up straight and looks him in the eye, ready to go on the offensive, he gathers. It's too late to recover from her moment of panic, and Travis already knows the answer.

"Well, this is rich," she says. "My husband's been murdered, and you want to come in here and turn this into something sordid? You should be ashamed of yourselves. Why would you say such a thing?"

Sloane narrows her eyes on Claudia. "Because that DNA we told you about? It was found on a pair of red thong underpants that belong to Daisy Parker."

Her eyes widen. "Are you insane? My husband and that . . . mousy little hippy girl? He would never be with a woman like that. Let me see the photo again."

Travis hands her the phone.

"No." She shakes her head. "There is no way my husband had an affair with that woman. I don't believe it. It's ludicrous. There must be some other explanation."

"Getting back to my original question, Claudia. Because you didn't answer me," Travis says. "Was your husband having an affair?"

"Keep in mind," Sloane adds. "If you know anything about an affair and we find out later that you knew, that could be a problem for you."

A voice calls down from upstairs. "Mother! Don't say another word!"

Gavin Mitchell comes barreling down the curved mahogany staircase, dressed in tan khakis and a navy polo shirt. Water droplets fly off his damp, dark hair and onto the hardwood floor. He rushes over to us.

"What did I tell you about talking to the police without me?" Gavin says.

"You know my son, Gavin," she says.

He's a thin man with a slight build and dark, deep-set eyes. He is of medium height, but he appears shorter with his hunched stance, like an old man waiting to happen.

"Hello, Counselor," Travis says. He has a vague memory of Gavin as a toddler, but he hasn't seen much of the adult version over the years.

"Why are you here, harassing my mother, instead of out there," Gavin gestures to the door. "Looking for my stepfather's murderer?"

"We're not harassing your mother. We're keeping her in the loop," Sloane says.

"Keeping her in the loop about what? Anything you can say to my mother, you can say to me."

"Yes," Claudia says. "Please tell my son everything you told me."

Travis fills him in on the latest happenings: the DNA and the red underpants they found on the boat, belonging to Daisy Parker, a radical environmentalist. The same woman who threw a brick through Kate Breslow's window.

Claudia looks at her son. "Your father was *not* having an affair with that woman. There has to be another explanation."

"Is she part of that new radical group? I forget the name." Gavin asks.

"The Shoreline Liberation Front? We think so. We're planning on speaking to them," Sloane says.

"Maybe they're behind this," he suggests.

"She wasn't having an affair with my husband," Claudia repeats.

"Maybe that group is behind it, and they're trying to frame her," Gavin says.

A puzzled look comes over his face as if he's realized the inherent contradiction in what he said. The same realization Travis has already come to. If the group was behind the murder, why would they leave evidence behind that implicates one of their own members?

"Anything's possible, but I doubt it was her own group that framed her."

"So," Gavin asks. "Do you have any other leads?"

"Oh, Counselor. Surely you know better than that. We can't comment on an ongoing investigation. Speaking of which, we need to get going."

Gavin holds out his card. "Please keep me in the loop."

Travis takes the card, and they head out.

As they're walking to the car, Sloane turns to Travis. "Doug Mitchell was Gavin's stepfather? Not his biological father?" she asks.

"Sort of. Doug Mitchell's not their birth father. He died when the boys were in elementary school. But Mitchell adopted the boys when he married Claudia," Travis says.

"But Gavin called Doug Mitchell his stepfather," Sloane says. "Maybe there was some friction between them, especially if the man was cheating on his mother."

"We could look into their estate plan. See if Gavin and his brother stood to gain anything from Doug Mitchell's death," Travis says. "Doug Mitchell was having an affair with someone; that much is clear. That could piss off Claudia. Or either of her sons."

"Gavin lives in Saugatuck," she says. "Think that's a coincidence? He's not stupid, though. Why would he dock the boat where he lives?"

"It's a good place to dock the boat if you don't want to be noticed. It's busy, with visitors coming in and out. And the slip they used is in exactly the right spot to avoid the cameras. Whoever did it knows this area. Knows boats. We need to look into the slip's owner. See if anyone knew him. Knew he'd be away for a few days."

"Where's the other son?" she asks.

"He lives in LA."

"So, any of the Mitchells could have a motive for murder. But how does Daisy Parker fit into all of this? Because as far as I can figure, she doesn't," Sloane says.

"I don't know yet. But there's an explanation. We'll get there," Travis says. "Let's go have another run at Parker."

———

"Are you out of your mind?" Daisy Parker pushes back from the table and springs up, holding her head in her hands.

"I think you should sit down, Daisy." Her public defender, a middle-aged man named Harry Beam, seems a bit out of his league, and Travis can't say he blames him. This started out as a vandalism case, and now she's looking at murder.

"I've never even met Doug Mitchell!"

"Daisy," Travis says. "Please sit."

He pats the tabletop in front of him, where she'd been sitting before she shot up like a jack-in-the-box.

"We want to hear your story."

She takes a deep breath and sits back down, obviously completely thrown by this revelation. "I already told you my story. Ryan Breslow and I were in love. And I have no idea how those got on Doug Mitchell's boat."

"They're yours?" Travis asks.

Daisy looks to her attorney.

They take a moment to confer.

"They look like mine. Yes. But I can't say for sure," Daisy says.

"My client has an alibi," Harry Beam reports. "She was at work all day, and then she was at a meeting with several other people who can corroborate this information."

"What kind of meeting?" Travis asks.

"An environmental group meeting," the attorney says.

"Which environmental group?" Travis asks. "The same one that condoned throwing a brick through Kate Breslow's window?"

"Last time I checked, we had a constitutional right to freedom of assembly in this country," Beam says. "And she's already confessed to the vandalism. There's no need to bring up the Kate Breslow incident. It has nothing to do with this."

Daisy leans over and whispers something to her attorney.

"Go ahead, Daisy. Tell them what you told me."

"Someone's obviously trying to frame me. We fooled around at their house a few times. Maybe I left my underwear over there. I'm sure Kate Breslow knew about the affair. It's probably her. Jealous wife, you know? Maybe she wanted to be rid of Doug Mitchell and get back at me at the same time."

Travis takes this with a grain of salt. It's plausible, but then she'd be out to get Kate Breslow, regardless. Kate's an easy mark. If the Shoreline Liberation Front is behind this, they'll say whatever they have to say to get Daisy off the suspect list. But then he remembers what Sloane said.

*Femme fatale.*

He knows Kate Breslow's keeping something from them, but he still can't see her as a murderer. Maybe he's got a blind spot. It happens sometimes. He'll run it past Sloane.

"Write down the names of the people in your group who can corroborate your alibi." Travis hands her a slip of paper and a pen.

"What about Kate Breslow?" she asks.

"What about her?" Travis replies.

"Are you going to question her about this?"

"That's none of your concern."

"It certainly is my concern! She hated Ryan. Made his life miserable. He told me all about it. He was afraid of her, you know. Afraid of what she might do to him. She had everyone fooled, he told me. She's not what she seems. And now he's dead. How do you know she didn't run him off the road that night?" Her lip quivers, and she starts to tear up.

The attorney places a hand on Daisy's shoulder. "We've had enough for one day, Detective. If my client's not under arrest, we're leaving."

Daisy takes a deep breath and looks Travis in the eye, batting back her tears. "I loved Ryan very much," she says. "I had nothing whatsoever to do with Doug Mitchell's death."

"Noted," he replies.

He's interviewed a fair number of suspects in his day, and he believes that she's telling the truth about her feelings for Ryan Breslow. He's not ruling out anything on the Doug Mitchell case, though, and he's anxious to learn more about the Shoreline Liberation Front. Maybe Parker was sleeping with Doug Mitchell to get information out of him. Stranger things have happened. Or maybe she's being set up by someone else. Or perhaps she's a cold-blooded murderer and not as dumb as she seems.

Still, he intends to pay Kate Breslow another visit. Because in his mind, she's exactly the kind of woman that Doug Mitchell would have an affair with.

*And that would explain a lot.*

# CHAPTER 11
## KATE

awake to find myself rubbing my forearms vigorously with my hands and realize that I'm freezing cold. Something goopy and wet pushes into the space between my toes.

I look down.

I'm standing in mud.

*Perilously close to the edge of the bluff.*

My eyes widen. I gasp and take a few steps back. I turn to look behind me, and my heart races. A trail of footprints on the pavers stretches to my back door, illuminated by the motion lights in my backyard that pierce the black of night. I look down at myself, the spotlight shining on me. My sheer white nightgown is stuck to me, and my skin shows through the gossamer fabric. I'm wet, I realize. I look up at the night sky. It's drizzling, and I need to get back inside. But I'm still foggy, not quite grasping what's going on.

*How did I get here?*

Then it hits me. What must have happened. I head back to the house. My racing heart starts to slow, but the pounding in my chest is replaced with an uncontrollable shivering that rattles my bones. I get inside and lock the door behind me.

But then I remember the brick. And I think about the fact that somebody could have slipped into my house while I was outside. The alarm people are coming in a few days, but that does nothing for me now.

The chances are slim, I tell myself. But still. I look around, and I don't see anyone. Then it dawns on me that if someone wanted to kill me, they could have simply pushed me off the cliff. So, I head upstairs to take a hot shower before I catch my death of cold.

I haven't had a sleepwalking episode in decades, not since my father died and left me parentless, but I remember all too well what they feel like. I'm devastated. I wonder what triggered it. I had one of those feelings again last night before I went to bed. Like someone was watching me. That's nothing new, though, and it doesn't explain why this is starting up again.

I need to get ahead of it. It's dangerous. And suddenly, prison isn't my biggest fear. At least in prison, I wouldn't be able to plunge myself off an eighty-foot cliff, shattering my body into a thousand pieces on the rocky shore below.

I laugh out loud at the thought and wonder if I'm starting to lose my mind.

———

I'm dry and warm, but there's no way I'm going back to sleep. It's five minutes past three in the morning, so I decide to do some research. Maybe there are some new studies about the causes of sleepwalking. There must be something new in the field after all this time. My episodes started when I was about six, according to my dad, and tapered off about a year later. But they started up again in the wake of my father's death. That was over twenty years ago. I wonder what the connection is.

I brew a cup of coffee and open my laptop, but my mind drifts back in time. Not that far back. Not twenty years back. Back to my happy place with Doug. The only time I've felt content since I lost my dad. Perhaps Doug's death might be triggering the sleepwalking.

After that couple's dinner, but before our first committee meeting, Doug asked me to come for a spin on his boat. It would give us a vantage point I couldn't otherwise get, he said. It would make it easier to explain what he'd found and what he was thinking.

After we got out onto the lake and anchored the boat, the conversation reverted to where we'd left off when our spouses had interrupted us that night at his house. He asked me why I decided to become a child life specialist. In half a decade, Ryan had never asked me that question.

I wasn't sure how much I wanted to disclose. I took a deep breath and started. "When I was six, my mother was diagnosed with ovarian cancer," I said.

That revelation usually prompts a sympathetic head tilt, but not this time. Instead, he nodded, and then we were silent for a few moments.

"Mine, too," Doug replied. "Lung cancer, not breast. She was a smoker. I was twelve."

"So, you get it," I said.

"I get it. Unfortunately," he replied.

He didn't take my hand or try to comfort me in any way. We sat there, the boat rocking to the rhythm of the gentle waves, in comfortable silence. A part of me wondered if this was a tactic. Getting close to me so he could manipulate me about the shoreline revitalization. Because of Ryan, I had some serious trust issues, and my guard was up.

"So that's why you decided to go into the profession?"

"Not exactly," I said.

He didn't pry any further. "So, you were raised by your dad, like me?" he said.

"Yes. He died when I was nineteen," I said. "I was a freshman in college at Barnard."

Now I got the head tilt, which is why I rarely tell my story to people unless they press the issue. I'd rather be an enigma. I don't want people's pity, and I hate the fact that I can out-trauma almost everyone. It makes me angry. I haven't even told him the whole story yet.

"Kate. That had to be terrible for you. Can I ask what happened? Do you want to talk about it?"

I usually don't, but there was something comforting about the rocking of the boat. Plus, I figured I could help him feel better about his lot in life by comparing his to mine.

"He worked in finance. In Manhattan," I said. "Not a trader. A mid-level accountant."

A seagull shrieked overhead, shattering the silence. Our eyes traced its path as it flew close to the boat and dove into the ocean after its prey.

"I'm forty years old now," I continued.

Doug looked at me, puzzled.

Do the math," I said.

His eyes widened. "Wait. Did he work in the towers? On 9/11?"

"Yes."

"I don't know what to say."

"There's nothing to say. I wasn't the only one. There were

sadder stories. We had some gatherings with the other families in my dad's firm. There were so many little ones. Robbed of their childhoods. I had to find a way forward. And that's when I realized I wanted to work with kids who'd been traumatized. It took me a while to find my exact career path. As I said, I was only a freshman when it happened."

"Shit, Kate," he said.

I smiled. It was a refreshing response.

Then he changed the subject back to the shoreline project. The area near the collapsed stairway had been cleared, but it stood as a stark reminder of how precarious the situation was. Doug pointed out spots where the bluff had deteriorated, and he went into some detail about the engineering behind some of the solutions. I felt like he was testing me to see if I could hold my own. I could, and he seemed impressed, especially with my willingness to have a conversation about it and not get emotional, like his wife or my husband.

It took months for our relationship to move into the physical realm. I pored over psychology texts, trying to make sure I wasn't getting duped again by my hormones. I'd slept with Ryan on the second date, and look where that had gotten me. I knew the hold I had over Doug, though. He wanted me, and I held out. He got to know me. Really know me. And when I gave in, I knew he was mine forever.

I go back to my laptop and search for studies on the causes of sleepwalking. I see the usual. Medications and alcohol, which I haven't used much lately. Stress. Sleep deprivation. PTSD, which my therapist thought was the cause of my episodes back when I lost my father.

I'd long since outgrown my childhood sleepwalking phase by the time I was in college, but the episodes started up again after his death. It was a terrifying day in Manhattan, and it seemed like an eternity before anyone knew what was happening or if we'd get attacked again. The fear combined with losing my only parent strained me, my therapist said, and the sleepwalking was my mind's coping mechanism.

A study jumps out at me. It's an older one, but one I've never seen before, linking sleepwalking to guilt. I click on it and start reading. Because I do feel guilty about something. I haven't told a soul about it.

*And I'm afraid it might drive me insane.*

———

"I can have ice cream for breakfast? Not an ice pop?" Braden looks at me, confused. "My mom said ice pop. But you said ice cream."

His mother's gone out of the room to get a coffee, leaving us to bond. I'm trying to gain his trust, so I don't want to contradict what she told him. I can't imagine that she would allow an ice pop and not ice cream.

There's so much packed into each sentence with children, especially when they're being prepped for surgery, so I have to read between the lines.

*Is he testing me?*

*Is he genuinely confused?*

*Is he trying to distract himself from his fears?*

"Well, the doctor says either one is okay. But I suppose it's up to your mom. What do you like better?"

He offers me a mischievous, elfin grin and rubs his hands together. "Ice cream! Can you tell her when she gets back? So, she knows it's okay?"

"Of course," I say. "What's your favorite flavor?"

"Cookie Dough," he says with confidence. I picture him as a leader on the playground, the kind of kid who gets his way but not a bully. Just an uninhibited, carefree little boy who knows what he wants. He's got dark brown hair in a bowl cut that's in need of a trim, and he periodically bats the bangs from his eyes.

"Oh, that's a good one. I like chocolate chip, myself."

This is my first case in over a year. A five-year-old boy going in for a tonsillectomy. After Ryan's accident, I removed myself from the on-call list and closed down my practice, which had practically deteriorated anyway. I wasn't experiencing grief in the way a wife normally would. It was a loss, though, and it hit me harder than I would have expected: the death of my marriage and a fantasy life I never got to have. I didn't feel I had much to give. About a month ago, I decided to start up my practice again, and I put myself back on the list. I'm grateful for the fact that this is an easy one.

I don't want to think about the tougher cases I've had. The terminal ones. The ones enduring unmanageable pain, the haunted look in their hollowed-out eyes. We're supposed to be honest with kids. Find ways to explain to them, at their level, what's happening and why. And what to expect going forward. But even most adults can't comprehend their own mortality, and many never come to terms with it. So how can we be expected to explain something this illusive to a child? That's the job I signed up for, though, and today I'm happy about that.

Because this, I can explain. I tell Braden that those pesky sore throats he's been having will go away, although it will get worse before it gets better. That's where the ice cream comes in. We talked about anesthesia, and I'm not sure he quite gets it, but I've convinced him that he'll sleep through the operation.

Now I show him the mask and explain how they'll put it over his nose and mouth. He shrinks back from me, shaking his head no.

*A common reaction.*

I pull out my tool kit and flash him a smile. "Braden. Check this out."

His deep brown saucer eyes follow my hand as I drip some liquid from a bottle into the mask, hold it in front of my lips, and blow. Squeals of delight emanate from him as he claps his hands, watching the bubbles float up into the air.

"Can I try it?" he says.

"Of course."

He gives it a go, blowing a stream of bubbles out of the mask, and soon we're laughing and playing and batting them around the room, and he's forgotten all about the fact that a mask like this will soon be used to put him to sleep.

His mother comes back to the pre-surgery room, and it's almost time for them to separate. This part can be tricky. That's why I like to bond with them first, because I'll go into the operating room with him and stay until he puts on the mask and starts breathing.

I explain this to him.

"Will you be there the whole time?" he asks me.

"No." I don't lie, even though he'd never know the difference. "But I'll be there when you wake up."

He nods.

"Ready to go?" I ask.

"Wait!" he calls out, and his eyes widen.

I'm concerned he may be having second thoughts. Some do. It's not that, thankfully. He asks his mom for confirmation that he can have ice cream for breakfast. Cookie Dough, he adds.

"Of course, sweetie," she says.

"Ready?" I ask.

He nods tentatively.

"I'll see you soon," the boy's mother says, and they're both starting to get choked up.

"Check this out, Braden." I squeeze the light-up toy in my hand, distracting him. He flashes me that grin again like we're sharing a secret. "Want to freak some people out while we wheel you in?

His eyes light up. "Okay," he says. "See you later, Mom."

He takes the toy from my hand and squeezes it as we start to wheel him into the operating room. His mother catches my eye and mouths *thank you,* and I feel a sense of satisfaction I haven't felt in way too long.

# CHAPTER 12
## TRAVIS

"Claudia Mitchell has a prenup," Sloane informs Travis. "It stipulates that in the case of a divorce, her husband gets next to nothing. But according to her trust, in the event of her death, control of her estate passes to her husband. After both of their deaths, it passes to her two sons, to be split evenly."

"We need to have another talk with Gavin Mitchell," Travis says. "Check out the brother, too. We only had one person verify that he was in L.A. that day."

"Quirky little guy, that Gavin Mitchell," she says. "How well do you know him?"

"Not well," Travis says. "I barely knew him as a kid. He lived in Boston for a while after college. Moved back a few years ago. Single. Aside from that, I know what you know. He lives in Saugatuck. He's an attorney."

"What about the other son?"

"Cory Mitchell works in the film business in L.A. Some sort of mid-level executive. Married. No kids. Doesn't come back here much."

"What did you find out about the owner of the slip? Any connection to the Mitchells?" Sloane asks.

"Nope. Not that I've found so far. He claims he doesn't know any of them. He's a weekender. Based in Chicago. Comes here frequently, but doesn't have any roots in the area."

"We need that damn toxicology report," Sloane says.

"I'll call over there. See if we can put a rush on it."

It's been over a week since Doug Mitchell's death, and although they've gotten the preliminary tox screen, the detailed report takes time. And that's critical to the investigation. They need to know exactly what was in his system, how much of it he was given, and how it got there to figure out who could have drugged him. Claudia Mitchell swears her husband wasn't taking any prescription sedatives, but then she might not know everything.

"So, it's someone who knows the area with access to benzos. Maybe someone who wanted him to miss the vote that night? Not kill him?"

"Could be. Maybe it was an accidental overdose. Someone drugged him to knock him out, but gave him too much."

"Someone makes a mistake and then conveniently has Daisy Parker's thong to plant?"

Travis lets out a sigh. "Maybe we're overthinking it. Maybe Daisy Parker seduces Doug Mitchell to get him to miss the meeting, some sort of directive from her organization. She screws up and dumps him in the lake in a panic. Then she cleans up but doesn't look under the cushions and misses the panties. Stranger things have happened."

"Sure. It's all on the table. But you know who would have a motive to frame Daisy Parker?"

"I do," Travis says.

"We need to take another run at Kate Breslow," Sloane says.

"I'd like to wait if that's okay with you. Dig around a little. See if we can find any evidence that she was sleeping with Doug Mitchell. If Kate Breslow thinks we've backed off her, she'll be more likely to slip up. Less likely to try to cover her tracks."

"Not too long," Sloane says. "She might skip town. There's nothing holding her here anymore."

"Good point," Travis replies. "I'll go check out Daisy's alibi. You stay on Kate Breslow and Gavin Mitchell. We can meet back up here later."

———

Luke Jenkins is not at all like Travis pictured him. His hair is short and neatly trimmed. Thick, black hipster glasses sit on the bridge of his nose. He's dressed in khakis and a navy polo shirt, presenting more like a computer geek or a scientist rather than the head of an ecoterrorist organization who would resort to murder.

He's an environmental scientist, close to forty, with a tenure-track position at a local community college, who introduced himself as Professor Jenkins. They're meeting at a diner-type establishment a few towns south of Crest Lake, near his home.

"You said you had some questions for me," Jenkins says.

"Daisy Parker claims that she was at a meeting with you and several others on the night of September fifteenth."

"That's a statement, not a question," he says, with a smug look on his face.

Travis glares at him. "Is this how you want to play it?

Because I'm investigating a murder, and this isn't a social call."

Jenkins leans in. "And I'm trying to prevent the murder of humanity. Crest Lake Township is living in a fantasy world. We should take a clue from the Europeans. They're taking it to a whole new level, and that's what we need here. Climate change is an existential threat to humanity. The greatest we've ever seen."

"Do you want to answer my questions here, or would you like to take a field trip to the station? Maybe it'll be good publicity. Drum up support for your organization. I could make it dramatic. Rough you up a little. Slap on the cuffs a little too tight so they can see you wince."

Jenkins takes a deep breath, looking off to the side. He sits back and folds his arms over his chest. "Okay. Daisy was with us that night. Yes. We were having a meeting. Last time I checked, we had the right to peaceably assemble."

"Where?"

"That's none of your business."

"It's *literally* my business. I'm a detective, and I need to establish a timeline."

Jenkins rolls his eyes. "We were at the college cafeteria. In Holland. Some of my students wanted to join us. A dinner thing. Well, not everyone was eating. It was sort of—"

Travis holds up his hand. "What time did it start and end?"

"It started around four and ended at about six-thirty."

"What were you meeting about?"

He goes on to explain that they were meeting about the shoreline vote, deciding on a strategy for whichever way it went.

"We're not the criminals, Detective. The Mitchells are the criminals. Putting up a seawall. Killing the ecosystem."

"So, you're glad Doug Mitchell is dead?"

He sits up and leans in again. "You don't get it, do you? We're law-abiding citizens. We've tried to be patient and work through the system. But the time has come for action. Have you seen what's happening in Europe? Does the name 'Just Stop Oil' mean anything to you?"

It does. They're the ones who threw paint on a Van Gogh painting and glued themselves to the streets to call attention to climate change. He's not in the mood for a lecture, though, or an indoctrination.

"Stop with the theatrics. So, you were meeting about the shoreline? Who was there?"

"Daisy Parker. Other group members. Some of my students."

"I'll need a full list of everyone who was at that meeting."

"I'll consult with my attorney on that. I'm pretty sure you need a warrant."

There's a pause, and Travis keeps his eyes trained on Jenkins until he looks away. He's right about the warrant, though, so he changes the subject. Throws him a curveball.

"How well did you know Ryan Breslow?"

Jenkins' jaw stiffens. "What does he have to do with this?"

"I'm asking the questions here," Travis says.

Jenkins rolls his eyes again. "I'm getting a little tired of this."

"Right back at ya," Travis says.

Reaching for his cuffs, Travis places them on the table and runs a finger along the smooth metal, watching Jenkins' eyes trace its path. Travis can see the man's neck start to twitch.

He's not the kind of guy who would hold up well in an interrogation.

"Not very well. He came to some meetings. We used his photography to help advance our cause. He seemed a little . . . full of himself."

"What was his relationship to Daisy Parker?"

"Humanity is on the verge of extinction, and this is what you want to focus on? The lives of a few people in some Podunk town in the middle of nowhere? This is meaningless, with all that's at stake."

"Spare me the *Casablanca* monologue and answer my question."

"I don't know what you expect me to—"

Travis pushes the cuffs towards Jenkins' side of the table. "Or do you want to take that field trip? It'd make for some dramatic headlines. Maybe even in Europe. You'll be a hero. Isn't that what you want?"

Jenkins looks down at the handcuffs and then back up at Travis.

"I think they were an item," he says. "But I wasn't too close with either of them on a personal level. She brought Breslow to a few meetings, and they came and left together. And that's all I have to say about it.

"But here's a warning to you, Detective. We're just getting started, and we'll do everything in our power to get what we want. Civil disobedience is our right and our responsibility. Property damage is on the table. But we're not murderers. And we don't go after people. We're trying to *save* people, not hurt them."

Jenkins strikes Travis as an armchair activist. One shove at a rally, and he'd likely be hightailing it back to his ivory tower to write a paper about it.

*But then, you never know.*

"I don't think you have it in you. And here's a warning to you. *Professor.* This is a murder investigation. Someone's going down for this, along with whoever helps them get away with it. So, think long and hard about my inquiries, and get back to me if anything else comes to mind. After you've had ample time for some . . . scholarly reflection."

Travis grabs his cuffs off the table as he stands, letting them dangle from his fingers as he turns towards the door and slowly exits the café.

# CHAPTER 13
## KATE

A week has passed since the sleepwalking episode, and I haven't had another one, at least that I can remember. That doesn't mean I'm in the clear. They're usually sporadic. Often, a sleepwalker will simply go back to bed, unaware of the fact that they've been out and about, unless something startles them like the bitter cold I felt the other night.

To ensure my safety, I now lock my bedroom door from the inside when I sleep, and I added a chain lock further up. High enough that I need to use a step stool to reach it. Now that the alarm is installed and activated every night, in the unlikely event that I'm able to get out of my bedroom, walk downstairs, and go outside, the blaring alarm will wake me before I can send myself tumbling down the bluff to my death.

There's been no further news on Doug's case. No further visits from the detectives. I know from experience that doesn't mean much. This isn't over, and I'm sure it's only a matter of time before they find out about Doug and me if they haven't already. I wonder about Claudia and if she could have possibly figured out what we were planning.

Doug and I both had burner phones, and I have no idea where Doug's is or if the police got hold of it. If they have, then they know everything, and I'm sure that would have prompted another visit. So, I can only assume that nobody's found it yet, or that Claudia found it and she's keeping it to herself for some reason.

What would she do if she found out about us? Not only about the affair, but about what we were planning? Would she kill her own husband? That seems hard to believe. She has so much to lose. She's holding all the cards. Why wouldn't she simply divorce him?

Then I think about her jabs at me. The snide remarks. I reflect on what Margaret said. *Claudia's the puppet master.* A control freak who has her family wrapped around her finger. If she felt betrayed, perhaps that could prompt a fatal reaction.

I'm alone in my bedroom, but for some reason, I look around before I open the flip phone to make sure nobody's watching me. That feeling still haunts me, most nights, that someone's here. It's funny how your imagination can be your own worst enemy at times like this.

This burner is my only remaining link to Doug, and part of me knows I should get rid of it. It's proof of our affair. We didn't use our names. And if they find his phone, I can always deny that it was me he was talking to. At least it's proof of what we were planning, and as long as I have it, it shows that he was worth more to me alive than dead.

Reading through the messages, I try to imagine what Detective Whittaker or Claudia Mitchell would think if they got hold of his phone. There are the usual steamy texts you'd expect from two people having an affair.

**Can't wait to see you.**

**Miss you like crazy.**

**I need you. Tonight.**

Nothing to indicate that it's me on the other end. No eye color or hair color. No distinguishing descriptions. Of course, no names.

But then there are the other texts. The ones about the bluff and our plan to double-cross Claudia. We thought it was funny. A double entendre that we couldn't quite get right. Operation Bluff, we called it.

**You'll sue me?? A little dramatic.**

**Operation Bluff tonight.**

**Ready for the vote?**

Those last two texts were sent a few hours before the vote. He didn't reply, which was unusual, but I figured he was with his wife and couldn't get to the burner. Doug was planning to leave Claudia, but only after we pushed through the vote for my plan. He had a prenup, and we wanted to secure the future of my home so we'd have the financial freedom to sell it and move on. It's not as if he was penniless. He had a substantial retirement plan and made a good living in insurance sales, but the home he lived in was all hers.

I'm making it sound like he was a bad person, but really, he wasn't. He knew that they were playing a dangerous game, hanging all their hopes on that seawall. Their home needed to be pushed back for their safety and for the safety of everyone below, and his wife's stubbornness could get someone killed.

Even if the board voted to extend the seawall across the length of the bluff like Claudia wanted, it would probably not get past the layers of government bureaucracy that would need to sign off on it. He honestly felt that my plan was the best one. The one that would secure her home, as well as the rest of our homes.

Doug's opposition plan was for show. A fake-out, if you will. Where we would make all kinds of threats to each other on our group text and at the committee meetings, but only to keep Claudia in the dark and buy us some time.

In the meantime, Doug was cultivating a client list back in New York so that after the vote went my way, we'd have an exit strategy. After pushing through my plan with his support that night, we planned to come clean to the board. He'd tell Claudia everything, and we'd leave town shortly after to start our life together. I could leave, even before the bluff work was completed, as soon as they started on the construction because that would be enough to allow a new buyer to insure it or get a mortgage.

I think back on that last text I sent to the group chat on my regular cell the evening before he drowned. About twenty minutes earlier, he'd threatened to sue me. I smiled and responded with the text that Whittaker already saw, the night Doug went missing.

**If you do that, I'll bury you.**

First, I imagined him smiling at our inside joke. Then I worried that the exchange was too melodramatic. That perhaps people would figure out it was a ruse. How was I to know our little charade had gone way too far, possibly implicating me in a murder?

When Doug didn't show up to the meeting, later that night, I knew immediately that something was wrong. After all, I'd texted him earlier. *Twice.* He hadn't answered, which was unusual for us. I hate to admit it, but the first thought that popped into my head was that he'd changed his mind. That his wife had somehow convinced him to stick with her plan. That he'd double-crossed me.

That doesn't even make sense, I know. Why wouldn't he simply show up and try to push his opposition plan through if he'd turned on me? That's how completely and royally my late husband had fucked up my head. I didn't trust anyone anymore. I didn't even trust my own judgment. I knew in my bones that Doug was mine, though, so that thought was quickly replaced with another one. A fear that he'd gotten into a car accident. It was a dark and rainy night, and he sometimes drank in the afternoon. Not in a million years did I expect that he'd been murdered on his boat. Pushed overboard and left to drown in the massive body of water.

Everyone in this town perceives me as his nemesis. If I come clean about the affair, it'll look worse for me in terms of Ryan's accident. But if I don't, I'm in the crosshairs for this one. Looking over the messages on my burner, it's clear to me that if anyone finds Doug's secret burner phone, they'll know it was me he was texting, and they'll figure out what we were planning. It's only a matter of time.

I only have one move. I'll go to Whittaker, using this burner as my evidence. I'll tell him everything, and then he'll know I had nothing to gain from Doug's death and everything to lose. And maybe he'll back off and put his focus where it should be. On the Mitchell family. Or the Shoreline Liberation Front.

*Anywhere but on me.*

I've had enough, and I need to go on the offensive and get my life back on track. I can't let fear and insecurity rule me any longer. I'll do it tomorrow after tonight's vote. Gavin Mitchell is surely using his influence to sway the undecided to Doug's plan or push some of my converts back his way. In the wake of his death, they may have second thoughts and want to support him out of sympathy for Claudia or respect for Doug's memory.

That's out of my hands, though. Rather than ruminate, I focus on drafting a plan. A way out. Trying to figure out how I can get this house sold and leave this place behind.

———

There's a slight drizzle tonight. On and off. The kind where you can't get the wiper speed right. The screeching of rubber against dry glass pierces the cabin, startling me as I pull into the parking lot of the town center. The rain has let up now, so I get out of my car, leaving my umbrella on the passenger seat.

I close the car door. It's dark and foggy, and I can barely make out the building across the parking lot from me. A woman comes at me out of nowhere. She's small, but in her crazed state, she looks terrifying. Instinctively, I shrink back, giving her the upper hand.

She wags a craggy finger in my face, her straggly hair casting a shadow over her features. As she comes closer, I see that it's Daisy Parker, looking like the Wicked Witch of the East.

"I know what you did!" she hisses. "I know who you really are! Ryan told me all about it. If you know what's good for you, you'll go in there and get those rich bastards to move their homes back and stop your plan from moving forward."

I catch myself and straighten up. I'm taller than she is, and she backs up a little. Then I lean in, pointing back in her face. "You listen to me, Daisy. I'll call the police if you don't get in your car and back off. *Now!* You already vandalized my home. I could have you arrested."

Grabbing my wrist, she pulls me in. She's surprisingly strong. "You're not getting away with this. I know you did something to Ryan, and I'm going to prove it," she says.

I break away. "Go. *Now!* Or I'll call the police."

"This isn't over," she says.

I shake off the interaction as she storms off into the mist. Taking a deep breath, I collect myself. I should call the police, but I don't want to be late for the meeting. I'll report it later when the vote is over. Rubbing my throbbing arm, I rush towards the building.

The mood is somber as I enter the makeshift board room for the second time in the last two weeks, still shaking. I'm a few minutes early this time. There are no new faces. Gavin Mitchell has yet to arrive. I make the rounds, shaking hands and greeting everyone, but we keep the small talk to a minimum.

The little feud between Doug and me had given the meetings a certain buzz. An air of intrigue, if you will. That's been replaced by melancholy over his death, tempered by an undercurrent of wariness. Someone was murdered, after all. Daisy Parker hurled a brick through my window. Collectively, we've gotten death threats.

A young man enters the room. From the photos I've seen at the Mitchell residence, I conclude that it's Gavin Mitchell. He's not at all what I expected. I thought he'd be brash and confident, like his mother, but he appears shy, almost painfully so, and nervous.

"Gavin," Sam Bolger says, walking over to greet him. "I'm the board president. I'm so sorry for your loss."

"Thank you," Gavin replies.

"Let's get you seated," Sam says.

He introduces Gavin. We all express our condolences. Soon enough, everyone will know the truth about Doug and me. I wonder what they will think of me and realize I need an exit plan. It won't go over well in a small town like this once I come clean to Whittaker and everyone finds out about Doug and me. Claudia has a great deal of pull here.

The board goes through the formalities of replacing Doug with Gavin. Sam makes a motion. Someone seconds it.

"All in favor, say, aye."

"Aye," the board members respond in unison.

Sam begins. "We're here to address—"

"Wait, please." Gavin holds up a hand. Before we vote, I'd like to make a statement," Gavin says.

"Of course," Sam replies.

Gavin stalls for a bit, his lips pressed. His eyes scan the crowd. After a few awkward moments, he starts. "Given the turn of events and the animosity towards the members of this committee, I'd like to officially withdraw my father's plan and back the compromise plan put forward by Kate Breslow."

I'm shocked. And judging by the number of raised brows in the room, it seems that I'm not alone. Perhaps the Shoreline Liberation Front is more of a threat than I thought.

Sam's brow furrows as he struggles to form a response. It's a rather unprecedented situation. "In that case, I'll be putting forward Doug Mitchell's plan in lieu of Gavin if there are no objections."

There's a prolonged silence. One of the board members winks at me as if to tell me I've got the numbers for it to go my way and not to worry. Sam waits another minute or two and then continues.

"You've all had ample time to review the two proposals.

On the matter of the vote for the shoreline revitalization plan for the township of Crest Lake, who is in favor of the plan put forward by Kate Breslow?"

Six hands raise.

"Who is in favor of the . . . alternate plan?"

Three raised hands.

*Two abstentions.*

I swallow.

The board passed my plan.

Rather than a feeling of excitement, a rush of fear washes over me as the realization hits me. Gavin's too afraid to push through the seawall plan. Two of the members are too frightened to vote at all. Now I'm the face of the plan that will go forward.

The fear of retaliation is soon replaced by a more pressing concern when we hear a knock at the door. It's Officer Alverson again. He strides in this time, visibly more confident, and my stomach sinks to the floor. Thoughts bounce around my head like ping-pong balls.

*Did Daisy Parker call them and try to claim I assaulted her?*

*Did they find Doug's phone?*

*Why didn't I consult an attorney?*

*Why did I wait so long to come clean?*

My heart's pounding in my chest so loud, I wonder if people can hear it. As he walks over towards me, I lean forward, preparing to stand. Then I stop myself because he keeps walking—towards Gavin Mitchell.

"Mr. Mitchell? I need you to come with me," the officer says.

The board member next to me grabs my arm, and I can only hope she didn't see me start to rise. We turn and glare at each other with wide eyes.

"What's this about?" Gavin asks.

"We'll discuss this at the station," he replies.

"Is this a request or a demand?" Gavin asks, with a resigned look on his face.

"It's a demand," the officer says. "Please. We need to go now."

With my plan secured and the spotlight off me for Doug's murder, I take a deep breath, slow my racing heart, and rethink my plan to come clean about the affair. All I want is to get out of this town, and with my plan moving forward, I can start on the revetment, cash out, and go. Forget about this town. Rebuild my life. Start out fresh.

*And never let another man control me again.*

# CHAPTER 14
# KATE


The house is not at all like I pictured it, but I don't want to burst Ryan's bubble. He lifts me up, carries me over the threshold, and places me gently on the dusty pine floor.

"What do you think, Kate?" His crystal blue eyes look back at me, a hint of trepidation in them.

"It's charming," I say, realizing that I can still back out of this.

We're engaged, not married yet, and I haven't totally committed to this move. This is my first visit. Ryan's from Oregon with no roots in the area, but he fell in love with this place on a photo shoot nearby, over a decade ago. He scooped up the property in the wake of the 2008 crash when prices plummeted. It's an eyesore, though, compared to the other lakefront homes, and I'm surprised he hasn't done more with it.

My best friend Holly thinks I'm crazy for even considering this move. We've only been dating a few months, and my child life practice is booming. Plus, I'm a city girl, she pointed out. And it's true. Manhattan's been my home since I was eighteen, but I'm ready for a change. When my father was killed in the tower collapse, my only remaining relative was my paternal grandmother, who lived on the Upper West Side. Not as far up as Barnard, but close. Nana, I called her. When school was out of session, I lived at her apartment, a cozy two-bedroom co-op with an elevator and a doorman.

She was a firebrand of a woman. Irish Catholic. Independent and strong, yet nurturing and wise. Without her, I'm sure I would have sunk even further down into depression. At the time, I was oblivious to the fact that she'd also lost a son, and I feel a bit insensitive for hogging the spotlight. Caring for me gave her purpose, though. We needed each other to heal, and I'm grateful that I had her. I met Ryan a few months after her death. As they say, when one door closes, another opens.

With my father's life insurance and the settlement from the victim's fund, I had more than a nice nest egg. But I would have traded it in a heartbeat to have my dad back. In my junior year, I paid off the mortgage on Nana's co-op and invested the rest, or what was left of it, after setting aside enough for four years of college tuition. The apartment is mine now, and I don't want to sell it. Renting a co-op is tricky, and Ryan is trying to convince me that it's better to cash out.

"You haven't seen the best part," he says. A tentative smile sits on his face, and I can tell he wants me to love it as much as he does. So far, I'm not too impressed, but I don't want to disappoint him.

He takes my hand and leads me out the back of the home. I suddenly get the appeal. The view is stunning. It's a late fall day, and the lake's shimmering surface stretches out as far as the eye can see. I've been to Chicago, so I knew Lake

Michigan was massive, but having it all to ourselves is positively magical. I wasn't prepared for it to be so rural, though. I'm not sure what I'd do to pass the time when Ryan's away on one of his shoots.

It's a long, winding drive up Lakeside to the top of the bluff, and we're higher up than I imagined. From this vantage point, it seems to go on forever, but it's a little freaky, being up this high. There's no barrier, and although it's not a cliff, the slope is dramatic. Ryan says the bluff used to have a gentler slope, but it's been worn down over the years at the toe, the spot where the waves hit it, making it more vertical.

There's a crescent beach down below, and the ten of us on our street share a staircase a few houses north of us, which gives us private access to it. It feels uncomfortable to me, the thought of having a beach to ourselves, being from Manhattan where most open space is shared by people from all walks of life. I wonder how the town's residents feel about that. There's a southern staircase that provides beach access to the public, but the northern part of the beach is now inaccessible due to erosion further south, including the beach in front of our home.

"Isn't it magnificent, Kate?" he says.

"Yes, it is," I have to admit.

"You're glowing. Let me get some shots." He picks one of the bright yellow daisies that dot the landscape here. He hands it to me. Then he grabs the camera that hangs from his neck and waves me over to the edge of the bluff.

I comply with his requests as he directs me.

*Turn this way.*

*Chin higher.*

*That's my girl.*

"I love the way your hair picks up the warm tones in the water. Wait till you see these, babe."

After a few minutes, he shows me his shots through the camera's viewer, and I hardly recognize myself. I'm stunning. I look like the happiest person on the planet. This place obviously becomes me.

*So what if the house is a little rustic?*

I think about the city. The noise. The grind. The rat race, rushing around from appointment to appointment, fighting for every inch of sidewalk. What would it be like? To have this much space and the freedom to simply . . . be? I turn and look out at the expansive view and realize that I could get used to this. Ryan wraps his arms around me from behind.

*It feels so safe.*

*So right.*

"You deserve a break, Kate. This doesn't have to be forever. We can fix up this place, cash out, and do whatever you want from there. Travel the world. Go back to New York, even if that's what you want. Although I don't understand the appeal. After all you've been through, I'd think getting some distance from that place would do you some good."

"Manhattan is my home. Everyone I know is there. My work is there."

That's not the only reason I stay. I'm not clueless. I know that living in a city that brought me so much tragedy could be viewed as a strange choice. Being around sick or dying children isn't exactly an uplifting profession. But moving away seemed to me like I was letting the terrorists win. I didn't want to give them that. I wanted to be brave and dedicate my life to something that mattered. Something that helped people move forward. Caring for others gave me purpose, but the thought of getting a respite from all of it is suddenly very appealing.

"Isn't it time for a change? Isn't there something else you've always wanted to do?"

"I suppose," I reply.

Before I lost my father, I wanted to be an architect, but I don't call attention to this, although I'm pretty sure I've mentioned this to Ryan. I'm not about to embark on that big of a career change, but remodeling this home seems like a fun project. Something to engage my creative side, and gradually, my fear of the unknown is replaced by excitement. I can put my career on hold. With Ryan's photography business thriving and my savings, we'll be fine.

"What do you have to lose, Kate?"

"Only everything," I say. "But what the hell? Let's do it."

He spins me around. The smile on his face reaches his eyes. They twinkle as he squints to shield them from the sun's rays. "You won't be sorry. I'll make you the happiest woman on earth."

"I already am," I say.

We sink into a long, lingering kiss that soon leads us back inside the house to christen it and celebrate the start of a new chapter in our life together.

———

Calling Crest Lake a small town is an exaggeration. A few blocks away from the stunning lakefront homes, there is another world. A world of local townspeople who struggle to survive in what's become a seasonal tourist town. Beyond that are acres and acres of farms, some prosperous and some not. And trees. So many trees. Tall ones of all shapes and sizes. Green and lush. Many of the lakefront residences are second homes and getaways for the wealthy. Movers and shakers or old money families in Chicago or elsewhere, sort of like a scaled-down version of the Hamptons. It's always been that way. As far back as the twenties. Some of the lakefront owners date back that far, while others are more recent.

I learned all this from a local woman at a bookstore, one of the few places in town of interest to me. There's also an upscale coffee shop, a locally owned general store, and a collection of eclectic small shops and businesses, but you need to head to bigger or more popular towns like Holland or Saugatuck for fine dining, a hair salon, or even a decent grocery store.

"And you've been here your whole life?" I ask the woman.

I forget her name, although she introduced herself when I brought my purchases to the counter: a history of the Great Lakes and a magazine on home remodeling. She's not quite as old as my grandmother would have been, but she reminds me of her.

"Most of it, yes. I was a teacher. I moved here from Seattle."

She tells me that she's retired now, and this job is only for fun. Keeps her busy, she says. I wonder if she's lonely. She's said nothing about a family.

"My fiancé has a home here. On the lakefront. And we're thinking about moving here for a while and fixing it up."

"Where are you from?"

"Manhattan," I say.

I tell her about Ryan's photography and how he's interested in the shoreline revitalization issue. She tells me there's some friction between the locals and the lakefront owners.

Some locals want to ban vacation rentals. And the shoreline has been shrinking over the years. There are some differences of opinion about how to handle that, she informs me.

"Are you sure you want to move way out here?" she asks. "Not much going on besides small-town drama, especially outside of tourist season."

"Is anybody ever sure about any major life decision?" I smile. "But I could use a change."

"I'm a little surprised, I have to say. A woman of your generation, moving for a man?"

"I'm not moving for a man."

Her eyes narrow on me. "Aren't you?"

She's smiling, but there's an edgy undercurrent to it. I shuffle my feet, a little taken aback by her candor. It's something my grandmother would have said. She'd try to talk me out of this move, for sure.

She rings up my purchase. "Do you need a bag?" she asks.

"No, thanks." I drop the book in my giant carryall and tuck my credit card in my phone case.

"Here. Take my business card. If you end up moving, stop around and pay me a visit. We can order anything you need, and you can pick it up right here."

I take the card from her.

*Margaret Brenner.*

"Thanks, Margaret."

"You remind me a little of my daughter. She's overseas now. Went with her husband to Germany."

The woman's probably lonely, and I'm a bit more understanding now about her comment.

"That must be hard," I say.

She shrugs. "It's life. You take care of yourself, Kate," she says.

As I turn and walk out of the shop, her words echo in my mind, and I could kick myself for letting her get to me.

I want a change.

I need a new adventure.

Life's short, and all that jazz.

I'm not moving for a man.

*Am I?*

# CHAPTER 15
# KATE


"You're moving for a guy?" Holly asks. Her wide eyes question my sanity. We're at a bistro near Bryant Park, and I'm back from my first visit to Michigan. The busy square is bustling with activity. Street vendors. Musicians. Business people grabbing their coffees. Tourists combing through the pop-up shops that spring up during the Christmas shopping season.

The buzz in the air is classic Manhattan, and my stomach sinks a bit as I think back on my stroll around Crest Lake, which seems like a ghost town by comparison. The bookstore and its lonely proprietor. The empty streets. But then, it was outside the tourist season. Perhaps I'll grow to appreciate the quieter moments, and I can always travel with Ryan if I get bored.

"What? No. I'm moving for a new adventure," I say. "I thought you'd be happy for me."

Holly and I have been friends since college, although with me, that doesn't mean much. I've had trouble getting close to people over the years. She tries to keep the friendship alive, and when we drift apart, it's usually on me. With my grand-mother gone, she's the only person I can trust to truly have my back. I know that this relationship with Ryan is moving at a brisk pace, which is why I asked her to have lunch with me. I wanted her input.

*So why am I bristling at her comment?*

"What are you going to do for work there?" Holly asks. She's a successful corporate litigator. Married with no kids. Her career means everything to her, and she's often tried to push me into a more lucrative profession.

I tell her about our plans to fix up Ryan's property. "Remember? This is what I've always wanted to do," I say. "I wanted to be an architect."

I was taking a class in modernity during my freshman year at Barnard. A multi-disciplinary course about what defined the modern era. One unit focused on the architecture of New York City as it ran out of space. It chose to rise higher and higher rather than accept the limits of its geographic confines, and the skyscraper was born. I found this fascinating. Who knew those very markers of modernity would become a target? After 9/11, I changed my mind and my major and never went above the tenth floor of any building.

She nods. "How's that going to work with your practice? Can you find enough work?"

"I might take a break from it. I have enough money saved. And they have hospitals there. I'm sure I can find work if I want it."

"Well, if this is what you want, I'm happy for you."

"Thanks, Holly." She says she's happy for me, but I can tell by the look on her face that she's concerned. That's only natural, and I think about what I would say to her if the situation were reversed. Would I be supportive or point out the fact that things are moving very quickly? They've never met, and I'd like them to, but so far, our schedules haven't matched up.

Our salads come, and I change the subject, turning the focus to her work. She doesn't push it any further, but I can tell she thinks this is a bad idea.

My phone rings. It's Ryan, and I excuse myself to answer it. He's frantic, wondering where I am.

"Kate! Where the hell are you?" he barks.

"I'm having lunch with Holly," I say. "I thought I told you that."

"No, Kate. I came home from my run, and you were gone. I've sent you like a dozen text messages. Why didn't you answer?" he says.

His forceful tone shocks me, making my stomach lurch. But then, I'm used to living by myself and not having to answer to anyone. I guess I need to work on being part of a couple. He's my guest, sort of. Maybe I should be more attentive.

"I . . . I'm sorry," I stammer. "I guess I forgot to tell you. I'll be home inside of an hour."

There's a prolonged pause, and my stomach tenses again.

*Why am I letting myself be put on the defensive?*

His voice softens. "No, I'm sorry, babe. I didn't mean to get so upset. I was worried. Anything can happen in this crazy city. I love you so much. If anything ever happened to you . . ."

I let out a breath and smile, pleased that he caught himself. "I love you too, Ryan. Don't worry. I'm a big girl. I can take care of myself."

"You've been taking care of yourself your whole life, Kate. Let someone take care of you, for a change."

My heart warms.

*He really does love me.*

"I appreciate that. Now, let me get back to lunch. I'll be home soon."

When I return to the table, Holly eyes me curiously. "What was so important?"

I explain that it was Ryan, and he was worried because I didn't let him know I was going out for lunch. I wasn't answering his texts. I can tell she thinks it's odd that he called, but she refrains from comment. But as I'm recounting the story to Holly, I realize something. Last night, I mentioned to Ryan that I was meeting Holly for lunch.

*Didn't I?*

*Or did I just think about telling him and forget?*

*Maybe I told him, and he wasn't listening to me?*

But Holly distracts me with a story about a new case she's working on, and the call slips to the back of my mind. I look around as she speaks, and I spy the entrance to the New York Public Library from my seat, one of my favorite spots to linger in midtown. It's a glorious building, full of history and knowledge. I'll miss this town, for sure. It doesn't have to be forever. Ryan wants to fix up the house and sell it, and then we can do whatever we want. The thought of that is exhilarating, and I'm looking forward to a change of scenery.

———

I get back to my apartment, and there's a bouquet of tulips waiting for me. My favorite flower. They're pinkish-red. Tight and fresh. Awaiting their full bloom.

"What's the occasion?" I ask.

Ryan brushes the hair back from my face. We sink into a

steamy kiss that makes me quiver. "No occasion. I missed you, that's all."

"Is that it?" I ask.

"I feel bad about the way I overreacted." He shrugs.

"It's no big deal," I say. "Forget about it."

*It was a big deal, though.*

*And I'm pleased that he realized that.*

In retaliation, I didn't come straight home after my lunch date. I stopped and did some shopping for nearly two hours. It was a test of sorts. To see what he'd do if I didn't come straight home. He passed with flying colors. No text messages. No frantic calls.

"Let's order in tonight," he says. "I want you all to myself."

I remind him that we have dinner plans with another couple, an acquaintance of mine from work, and her husband. I'm looking forward to it, I explain. She and I hit it off, but our friendship has been mostly confined to work, with my being single. Married couples tend to socialize with other couples, and I'm excited to be part of one now.

"I'm leaving tomorrow, Kate. Could we cancel? Please? I need some downtime. And some alone time. With you." He brushes my cheek with his fingers and pulls me in for a kiss. It's been a commuter relationship for the past few months, and I'm the one who's been dragging my feet on this move.

*God, he's so hot.*

And he's right. We haven't had much alone time, between my work and my desire to show him off around town. He takes me by the hand and leads me into the bedroom. His sexy smile fires me up inside.

"Maybe we can try to break our record tonight," he says.

My body shudders in anticipation as his hands caress me,

his eyes hungry for me. He undresses me slowly, tracing his hands along my bare skin. He never takes his eyes off me, and something is intoxicating about that, like I'm the only woman on earth who can quench his desire. Soon, we're in bed, skin to skin, and all thoughts of what's outside this room vanish from my mind. His lovemaking is fun, exciting, and tender, all at the same time, and the sensations bombarding me are almost too much to handle. Soon, my body erupts in pleasure, and it's like an out-of-body experience.

"I love you Kate," he says, as he wraps me in his arms and kisses the top of my head. "You're not alone anymore. I've got you, babe. Forever."

"I love you too, Ryan." I snuggle into his warm embrace. We lay for a long while, spent and satiated.

Reaching for my phone, I fire off a text to my work friend. Something about a sore throat. I'm moving away. What's the point of cultivating that friendship, anyway?

"We have the night to ourselves," I say, telling him about my text and the feigned illness. "Think we can keep each other entertained?"

"Oh, babe. We're just getting started."

I burrow into his embrace, feeling like the luckiest woman on the planet.

# CHAPTER 16
## TRAVIS
### PRESENT DAY

Travis expects his suspect to lawyer up as soon as they get to the station. Instead, Gavin Mitchell uses his one phone call on his mother. He has something to disclose, he tells the detectives. Once she arrives, he says, he will explain everything.

Travis and Sloane try to rattle him, nonetheless, keeping the details vague and ominous. Travis doesn't reveal to Gavin exactly what they have on him: video footage of Gavin boarding his stepfather's boat about twenty minutes before it left the dock. A passer-by recorded it on her phone and turned the footage over to the police when she heard about the case.

Travis and Sloane attempt to grill him. See if they can get him to admit to harming his stepfather. Gavin doesn't flinch, though. Citing the Fifth Amendment, he declines to comment.

Leaving Gavin alone in the interrogation room, they observe him through the one-way window. He paces for a bit and then sits with his head in his hands. After ten minutes or so, he stands up and starts pacing again, and they can see that he's starting to sweat.

"He's nervous," Sloane says. "So why wouldn't he call a lawyer? And what the hell does his mother have to do with it?"

Travis shrugs. "Maybe we'll get lucky. What's the chance he comes clean right there in that room? Confesses to murder?" Travis asks.

"Probably zero," Sloane replies.

"Think he knows what we have on him?"

"I would assume. But if he does, it's even weirder that he didn't lawyer up."

"Maybe it's a strategy."

"How so?"

"Well, if he wants us to believe he's not guilty of murder. That he had some other reason to be on the boat, it could be a way to try to convince us he's innocent. By *not* calling a lawyer."

"What other reason could there be for him being there at the dock?"

"I guess we're about to find out."

Claudia Mitchell arrives, accompanied by a tall man with silver gray hair and wire-rim glasses, wearing a crisp suit that looks expensive and out of place in a small town.

"This is Fred Hastings. He'll be representing my son," Claudia says.

"I'll need a moment with my client," Hastings says.

Travis and Sloane comply with his request, and they wait outside with Claudia Mitchell, who seems surprised when she isn't asked to join them. Fifteen minutes later, they're called back in.

"What's this about?" Claudia asks Travis.

"Why don't you tell her, Gavin?"

"I have no idea what it's about."

"Oh, I think you do," Sloane says. "We have footage of you boarding your father's boat. The day he was murdered."

Claudia gasps. "There must be some mistake."

"No, it's true. I can explain, Mother," Gavin says.

"Go ahead, Gavin," Hastings says. "Tell your mother and the detectives what you told me."

"Mom, I need to tell you something before you find out from anyone else. And I'm warning you, it might upset you."

Claudia Mitchell glares at Hastings. "What's going on here, Fred? Why are you letting my son talk? Isn't that . . . ill-advised?"

Hastings peers at her over the top of his wire rims, stopping to adjust his glasses before he speaks. "Claudia. You need to trust me on this. It's not what you think."

She turns to Gavin. "Well, whatever it is, I'm here for you."

"Don't be so sure about that," Gavin replies.

There's an awkward silence, and then he continues.

"This evening, right before the detectives interrupted us, I withdrew my plan and voted for Kate Breslow's plan."

Claudia's jaw stiffens, but she keeps her voice steady and low. "You did *what?*"

"Mom. Hear me out." He puts his hand on hers. "I did it for you. For us. And for our future."

Gavin goes on to explain his position. Having their home so close to the edge of the bluff poses too much of a risk. He and his brother agree on this point. And Kate's plan is the only way forward.

Claudia speaks through a pair of pressed lips. "How

could you do this? Behind my back? You're my *son*, Gavin. And you're taking her side?"

"Yes, I'm your son. So, it's my job to look out for you. For us. You can't even get homeowner's insurance. It's too dangerous. For you. For everyone."

She turns from him with her hand on her chest. Then she curls into herself, and it seems to Travis that this is new information she's absorbing. Claudia addresses her son again. "Your brother too, Gavin? Both of you feel this way?"

Her son nods. "I'm sorry, Mom."

"This is all very entertaining," Sloane says. "Having a front-row seat to your family drama. But what does this have to do with Doug Mitchell's death?"

"We're getting there," Hastings says.

"Get there faster," Sloane replies.

Gavin turns to Sloane. "I went to my stepfather's boat that day to talk with him. To feel him out before the vote. To tell him how my brother and I felt about it." He turns to his mother. "And I'm sorry to tell you this, Mother. But Doug agreed with me. He told me he was going to withdraw his plan and back Kate's."

"So my whole family's against me," Claudia says.

"Let's do this later, Mother," Gavin replies. "I'm facing a murder charge here."

"Good plan," Travis says. It's not lost on him that Gavin referred to his stepfather by his first name when he addressed his mother. He didn't call him dad. Perhaps there was some friction between them, especially if Gavin knew about the affair.

Gavin turns to the detectives. "I had nothing to do with his murder. I was gone well before then before my stepfather even left the dock. I can prove this with the GPS from my car.

I was in meetings all day in Saugatuck, and I had a dinner engagement that night. Several people can confirm this. I'll take a lie detector test. Whatever you want."

"Why did you go to the boat to talk to him?" Travis asks. "Why not do it at home?"

Gavin takes a deep breath. "Because I didn't want my mother to know about it."

Tears well up in Claudia's eyes. She turns from them. But Travis isn't buying it yet. This whole thing could be an elaborate deception. They could all be in on it together. The mother and her two sons, who stand to inherit everything. They're likely not too keen on a stepfather who cheats on their mother.

"We'll take you up on that polygraph. And get us the GPS evidence you mentioned. And the names of the people who can corroborate your alibi," Travis says. "But Claudia. We still have a murder to solve. I'm going to ask this question one more time. And now that we know your son was on the boat, I'm going to need an answer. And if you don't give me one, I'll subpoena you."

"What do you want to know?" she asks.

"To your knowledge, was your husband having an affair?"

Claudia looks to her attorney. "Go ahead, Claudia. It's better to get it out in the open.

"Yes," she says. "But he was planning to break it off with her. He promised me after I confronted him that morning. The morning of the shoreline vote."

"Do you know who it was with?" Sloane asks.

Claudia nods.

"And?" Sloane asks.

"Kate Breslow. My husband was having an affair with Kate Breslow. He admitted it to me the day he was killed."

An officer interrupts the interrogation.

"Detectives? Can you come out here for a minute?" he says.

Claudia Mitchell wears a somber look on her face as they exit the room, and then she rests her head in her hands.

---

"We've got some unfortunate news," Travis says after he and Sloane reenter the interrogation room. "Take a look at this."

He pulls up some photos of their seawall. Bright red blotches of paint are splattered across the metal structure, like blood spatter at a crime scene. The words CRIMES AGAINST HUMANITY scream out in angry brush strokes, running diagonally across its surface. A group of ten or so members of the Shoreline Liberation Front pose in front of it, with Luke Jenkins smack in the middle. Daisy Parker's not in the photo.

"Oh my god!" Claudia's hand goes to her mouth. "When did they . . ."

"We don't know," Sloane says. "A squad car is headed there now. Did either of you notice anything before you left the house tonight? Any unusual activity in the area?"

"Not at all," Gavin says.

Claudia pauses, her head tilted to the side, looking deep in thought. "Wait!" she says.

They all turn to her.

"When I was out in the front yard, around four in the afternoon, I thought I heard some people on the beach. They sounded close, but I assumed it was coming from my neighbor's beach. They Airbnb the home to tourists, so I figured a new party had arrived. How would those terrorists have even gotten there? The public stairs collapsed."

Gavin jumps in. "They trespassed. Obviously. Are you going to arrest them?"

"How did you get this photo?" Claudia asks.

"One question at a time," Travis says. "The Shoreline Liberation Front sent it to us. And to the local news media. That guy in the middle's Luke Jenkins. The email came from his personal account. He's their leader. We're sending a car over to his place now."

"How do you know all this?" Gavin asks.

"I can't comment on an ongoing investigation," Travis says.

"But I'm the victim here!" Claudia says. "My home's been vandalized. My husband's been murdered. Gavin's explained why he went to the dock. Surely, you can see he had nothing to do with my husband's death. And I'm frightened now. Truly terrified."

"It's a complicated situation," Sloane replies. "But we'll keep you updated on the vandalism. Maybe you could stay somewhere else until we have more information?"

Fred Hastings places a hand on Claudia's shoulder. "It's a good idea. Perhaps you two could stay at Gavin's place for a few nights?"

Claudia looks at her son.

"I think it's a good precaution, Mother. I've got plenty of space."

"Is this what it's come to? I'm a refugee. In my own town!"

"Let's try to stay calm," Gavin says.

Claudia turns to Travis. "Get control of those radicals, Travis, before they ruin our entire way of life. And don't forget to have a talk with Kate Breslow. She's hiding a lot more than an extramarital affair, I'm sure of it."

"How about you take care of yourself and leave the detective work to us?" Travis says.

"Is my client free to go?" their attorney asks.

Sloane replies, "He is. For now. We'll be checking out Gavin's alibi."

"Don't leave the vicinity," Travis adds. "You can see yourselves out."

Claudia rolls her eyes, and they all exit the interrogation room. Once the three visitors are out of earshot, Sloane turns to Travis.

"Next stop, Kate Breslow's house?" Sloane asks.

"How's about first thing in the morning," Travis says.

"You don't want to go now?"

"Sure, I do. But only because I have no life. But you do have a life. And it's late."

"You sure?" she asks.

"Yeah, I'm sure. You don't want to end up like me. A lonely old goat."

"I wouldn't say you look like an old goat. More like a middle-aged one." She doesn't smile, and he can't help but wonder if she actually meant it.

"Gee, thanks."

Sloane shrugs. "Maybe lose the beard. And if you're feeling lonely, that new prosecutor was checking you out a few weeks ago. She's pretty cute."

"I have eyes, Sloane," he says. "I don't need your dating tips. Now go home to your husband before I change my mind."

With that, Travis shoos her out of the precinct, eager to have some quiet time to look over his case notes without all the distractions. Sloane's right about one thing, though. He could use some female companionship, but he's lazy about that sort of thing. When he was younger, women were every-where, and it wasn't that hard to keep himself occupied. Now that he's older, it's become more of a challenge. Maybe when this case is over, he'll put in some effort. For now, he opens a file and gets to work.

# CHAPTER 17
## KATE


Ryan's been distant lately. He goes out a lot without me. And he hardly touches me anymore. I have a feeling that he's cheating, but I haven't wanted to face it or confront him. I examine myself in the mirror, noticing all my flaws. My nose is a bit too long for my face. There's a pallor to my complexion. My lips appear deflated. I'm thin but not very fit.

There are no fancy gyms around here. I jog and hike when the weather permits, but I miss my exercise classes. It's the dead of winter, and I'm having a hard time keeping in shape. The winters are grey and long here. It's colder than in New York, and I'm starting to think I made a major mistake moving here. I've tried to make friends, but it's a bit cliquish, and the women my age haven't been very welcoming.

I think about calling Holly and going back to New York for a visit. It's been years since I moved, though, and I've lost touch with her. Admitting to anyone that I'm having second thoughts about my marriage will make it more real.

It's probably a phase.

All marriages have their ups and downs.

*Right?*

But a part of me knows this isn't normal. I scarf up the crumbs Ryan throws my way, ravenous for his validation. I'm not myself anymore, and I need to find my way back. I'm not ready to give up on my marriage, but I need a plan to be financially secure and get some power back in this relationship.

The renovation was much more expensive than I had projected. Prices shot up and supplies dwindled, dragging out the process. I persevered, and we're almost done. My child life practice has deteriorated, though. Over the years, Ryan's tried to convince me that it's bad for me. That it contributes to my depression.

But that's not true. Back in New York, my work gave me a sense of purpose. Being here, alone much of the time, that's what has depressed me. There weren't any full-time jobs available when we moved, so I started working as an independent contractor. With the renovation taking up most of my energy and time, I got distracted. I'm still on the on-call list for a few of the hospitals here, but I've said no a few times, and I'm afraid if I don't take more cases, they'll stop calling. So, I checked in with a few of them recently and let them know that I'm still available.

It's not a high-paying profession, though, even in the best of markets. I need to find a way to make some decent money because my nest egg has shrunk considerably. I sold my condo in New York like an idiot. I've done some research on the implications. The money is commingled now, and Ryan's entitled to half of it, whereas if I'd left it as an inheritance, he wouldn't have been able to touch it.

I ran my financial dilemma past Margaret, the one who

reminds me of my grandmother. She's pretty much the only friend I have here, but I didn't let on about my marital issues. She pointed out that it wouldn't take too long to get my doctorate in clinical psychology. I already have a master's degree, and there's a high demand for more therapists.

Margaret shared with me that she'd given up on her dream of becoming a doctor, instead choosing to support her husband while he attended law school by working as a high school science teacher.

"I thought that one day it would be my turn. But that day never came. Don't make the same mistake, Kate," she warned.

Although she's likely living vicariously, her suggestion was a good one. I found an online program with a clinical externship, and I can complete it inside of three years. I've enrolled, and I plan to use some of my remaining inheritance for the tuition. I need to tell Ryan about the decision. That thought puts my stomach in knots.

*But why?*

And I realize what I've been trying to deny.

The question I've been reluctant to ask myself.

*Am I afraid of my own husband?*

———

"What? I don't make enough money for you? Is that all you're about, Kate? Money?" Ryan paces around the living room. His fists are tightly balled, a vein bulging in his neck.

*What on earth is he talking about?*

"Ryan. Yes, we need to make a living. You haven't had a paying photography job in over a year."

"Oh, right. Put the blame all on me. Well, you're the one

who wanted to go all in on this home renovation, Kate. You built a whole new house! I never asked for that. This was your idea." He throws up his hands, dismissing everything I've accomplished.

*Why doesn't he appreciate all I've done?* The place looks spectacular. Everyone says so. I've quadrupled our money.

"We'll get it all back when we sell it, Ryan. And then some," I remind him. "We came to that decision together. Remember? We were planning to flip it, cash out, and leave. Do whatever we wanted with the rest of our lives."

He stops pacing and glares at me, his hands on his hips. "So that's what this is about. You can't stand it that I've made a life for myself here and you haven't. All you do is sit around here and mope. I mean, look at yourself, will you?" He looks me up and down, his face full of disgust. "I hardly recognize you anymore."

For a moment, I feel as if I might break down and cry, and I could kick myself for letting his words sting.

*Why can't I be stronger?*

Then I take in the sight of him. The clenched jaw. The pressed lips. He's containing it, but there's a rage seething underneath. He's holding it together, but barely. A wave of fear shoots through my body, energizing me, a welcome change from the lethargy. He's never been this bad before. He's been distant for the past year or so. Colder, sure. But not cruel.

I wonder what triggered this kind of reaction. Could it be the simple fact that I've defied him? One thing's clear to me now. There's something wrong with my husband, and I need to tread carefully. There's no telling what he might do.

I take a deep breath and straighten up, choosing my words carefully. My tone is firm and measured, but not aggressive. "Ryan. It's my money. And I'm sorry if this decision upsets you. You have a right to your opinion. But I've been accepted into the program, and I'm moving forward with my doctorate."

He attempts to stare me down, but I don't flinch or look away. My senses are on high alert, though. The fight-or-flight instincts have kicked in. There's a tense stand-off as my palms start to sweat. Finally, he starts for the front door.

"Do what you need to do, Kate. But I'm not selling this house."

He storms out, slamming the door so hard behind him, it causes the paintings on the wall to rattle. Soon, I hear his car start up and let myself take a breath. It was a gamble, standing up to him.

*But it worked.*

Then I start to tremble, letting myself feel the full weight of the visceral fear. Breathing through it for a few minutes, I try to slow my pounding pulse.

*How did it come to this?*

Then I steel myself, hardening my heart and strengthening my resolve. It's not the time for tears or regrets. I need action. So, I open my laptop and get to work. There's something wrong with Ryan. It's not me.

*And I'm going to figure a way out of this emotional prison.*

# CHAPTER 18
## KATE
### ONE YEAR AGO

*Narcissists can be charming and have a way of making you feel special, which can be extremely seductive.*

*The characteristics of this disorder include a need for admiration from others, a grandiose manner of relating, and a lack of empathy for those around them.*

*Narcissistic Personality Disorder can be classified into three sub-types—grandiose/obvious, vulnerable/hypervigilant, and high-functioning.*

*It can be difficult to tell the difference between a narcissist and a psychopath. All psychopaths are narcissists, but not all narcissists are psychopaths.*

I've always been a good student, and this time is no exception. This doctoral program has been a godsend in more ways than one. It's given me something else to focus on, sure. And a potential path forward with a higher-paying career when I finish. It's also practical, providing valuable information about Ryan and how to handle him. Because I'm not leaving without my nest egg, no matter what I need to do to get it. My first step is figuring out what's wrong with him, and my graduate seminar in abnormal psychology is helping.

As far as Ryan's diagnosis, my best guess is narcissistic personality disorder. At first, I thought Ryan might be a sociopath, but our professor says that sociopaths are generally not very personable or intelligent and that the term is often misused. I crossed that off the list and narrowed it down to psychopath or narcissist, but I'm going with narcissist. He checks more of the boxes for that, including his family history.

There are two theories as to what kind of family background fosters the development of a narcissist. Social learning theorists believe that overvaluing children is the root cause, whereas psychoanalytic theorists believe the opposite, that a lack of warmth or detachment from the child causes it. Ryan had both. A double whammy, from the little bits he's told me.

His father died before we met, but from what Ryan said, he was a control freak who lived vicariously through his son and didn't approve of his career choice. By contrast, his mother is cold and detached. So much so that she didn't even come to the wedding, citing work obligations. I've only met her once when we went to Oregon for a visit. She lives in a suburb of Portland, but we stayed in a hotel in the city, and she saw us only twice during the time we were in town. Like me, Ryan's an only child, and I picture his mother snapping her fingers at the OB the minute he popped out, ordering her to tie up those tubes. I wonder if Ryan was an accident, and if so, why she even went through with the pregnancy.

I'm not sure if he's the grandiose/obvious or the high-functioning type. Our professor said they could sometimes exhibit traits from all the subtypes at various times, but they'd normally have one that's a baseline. I'm doing my term paper on this disorder, killing two birds with one stone. Ryan's very private about his outlandish behavior, keeping his episodes close to home, so I'd probably go with high-functioning narcissism.

I hope I'm right, and he's not a psychopath, though. Because they look similar from the outside, especially when they're reeling you in: smart, successful, charming. There's a fine line between them on the surface. Still, the correct diagnosis is important because the strategies for how to approach a toxic relationship with a narcissist and a psychopath are different. I need to be sure before I launch a plan of action.

They both like to call the shots, so getting out of a relationship with either is hard. But while narcissists are often hurtful and manipulative, they aren't as likely as psychopaths to cross over into physical violence. The wrong approach could be deadly.

*So how does one tell them apart?*

My professor mentioned some key differences. Psychopathy is physiological, whereas narcissism is more of a learned behavior, although there's some debate about that. PET scans have revealed that psychopathic brains function differently than normal brains. The parts that control empathy don't engage or light up during these scans. I can't very well make Ryan get one, so that doesn't help me.

There are other differences, ones that are more difficult to parse out. Narcissists care what others think of them, whereas psychopaths don't. It's not an empathetic kind of caring. It's self-centered. They care about how others perceive them because they need to be put on a pedestal. To be adored. To feel special. This explains why Ryan looked to other women when his hold over me began to fade and why he's so enmeshed with the environmental groups that fawn over him and stroke his ego.

I've been trying some of the techniques she recommends for handling a narcissist, and it seems to be working so far. Those strategies are for people who want to stay in the relationship, not for people who want to get out.

*Set boundaries.*

*Have realistic expectations.*

*Radical acceptance—because they'll never change.*

But what about the people who want to leave?

I take a deep breath, close my computer, and think back on my relationship with Ryan, shutting off my intellectual side and tapping into my emotions. It's a weird feeling, psychoanalyzing your own marriage. At times, I feel detached, like it's happening to someone else. Then, a memory will surface, and it hits me in the gut.

The happy ones are worse than the terrible ones. Like earlier today, I glanced over at these two figurines on our mantel and thought about the time we bought them a few months after we moved here. We found the cutest little store along Blue Star Highway, filled with an eclectic collection of used household goods, antique furniture, and a variety of nicknacks. The proprietor was a chatty older woman around Margaret's age who knew the origin of almost everything in the store. She informed us that the figurines had come from a couple who had been married for over sixty years.

"Maybe they'll bring us good luck," I said.

"We don't need luck," Ryan replied.

"Aren't you two just the cutest?" the woman said. "You should have them. I have a feeling you'll continue their legacy." Then she offered us a discount on the figurines. It felt meant to be at the time, but she was probably just trying to make a sale.

I miss those days. I miss us and the way I felt when we met. And then I beat myself up for being such a wuss. And for the way he duped me. I'd read articles about women in toxic relationships and always wondered how they let it happen. Why didn't they simply leave? I know now that it's not that simple. Ryan loves me in his own twisted way, and that kind of obsessive, controlling love is quite the ego trip. And, of course, the change happens gradually, so gradually that you start to question your sanity. Then, before you know it, you're stuck.

---

"Hey there," Doug says as he walks through my front door, happy to see me, as usual.

I save my file, close my computer, walk over, and kiss him. Ryan finally got a paid photography job, and he's away on a shoot. We're at my house, and I know that's risky. It's winter, so it's dark outside, and he switches out his car with a rental, leaving his car a few towns over.

*But still.*

My relationship with Doug is making my time here much more enjoyable. At times, I feel content. Almost happy. We laugh. We enjoy each other's company. If my husband hadn't burned me, I'd probably be madly in love with Doug by now. Our backgrounds are similar, both having experienced loss and pain. Doug's wife is a controlling shrew, so we have that in common, too.

*Miserable marriages.*

We both want out. Our affair has become a refuge for both

of us, but I'm guarded, keeping my feelings at bay. It's nothing like it was with Ryan when we couldn't keep our hands off each other. I suppose that's a good thing, but I wonder if there's something wrong with me for not feeling more of an attachment to Doug. I hope my husband hasn't ruined me for life. I don't want to give him that kind of power over me.

"I opened a bottle of wine," I say.

We don't hop straight into bed. It's not like that. When we're together, it feels like this is my normal life. Like we're the married couple, and in my other life with Ryan, I'm playing a role. It's exciting, I must admit. Plotting my revenge right under my husband's nose. It's more exciting than my extramarital affair, and I wonder if there's something wrong with me. Doug brought over some takeout from an Italian place called Mario's, which is a few towns over. He hands me a white bag with red lettering on it.

"Smells delicious," I say. Truth be told, the Italian food here is nothing compared to New York. I don't say things like that to anyone, though. That's exactly the kind of comment that puts people off of newcomers.

I set it all out on the table and go into the kitchen to get some plates. He follows me, comes up behind me, and runs his hands up and down my sides, gently nuzzling my neck. It feels nice, and my body responds. I take that as a good sign.

It's fine. This is a normal relationship, I tell myself. I need some time to get used to it. Part of the process of disengaging from a toxic relationship is getting used to something healthy. We learn to like what's familiar, even if it's not good for us. I need to give it time and learn to accept Doug's unconditional love, even if it feels a bit flat right now.

"I'm more excited for dessert," he says.

But we don't rip off our clothes. Instead, we sit and eat, and start to discuss the new proposal I got from a contractor. The revetment will cost a good deal more than I had hoped, and they can't start on it for at least another year. His was the most reasonable bid, and the other contractors are also backed up. Lots of towns are having this problem. I need to run everything past the Army Corps of Engineers, and that's going to take some time. Doug and I decide that this bid is the one I should use in my submission to them.

Meanwhile, he's moving forward with his proposal, a combination of seawalls and sandbags. He shows me some evidence that the lake's water level has risen and fallen over the decades in a predictable thirty-year cycle. Lake Michigan's most dramatic rise was in 1986, and many homes were lost that year.

Then, in 2013, the lake was at a low point, and people were concerned that it would be catastrophic for shipping and transportation. If the lake's water level gets too low, the freighters can't take on as much weight, reducing their loads and increasing shipping costs. And with that, prices for consumers.

In 2017, the lake started to rise again, coming within an inch of its highest level, impacting municipalities in multiple states. That was about the time he and Claudia put up their seawall, which only furthered the problem for their neighbors, including us. When one property puts up a structure, it magnifies the problem for the other homes, and now we're all in the danger zone.

Doug continues. "If we extend the seawall, we can stop the erosion without reangling the bluff."

"I'm sorry. What did you say?" For a moment, I wonder if he's changed his mind about our plan to dupe Claudia.

He catches himself. "I mean, that's what Claudia would say. That's what she wants me to present in my plan."

"Very convincing. For a moment there, I thought maybe you'd switched sides."

"I'm not going to lie," he says. "It's tempting to believe it. Putting up a seawall, or even using geotubing and sandbags, is faster than reangling the bluff and constructing a revetment.

"True, but—"

He puts his hand on mine. "Which means we could be together sooner."

I smile. "We're together now."

"It's not enough. I want to be with you all the time."

My stomach tenses at the thought, and I realize that things are moving too fast with us. "We need to be patient," I say. "Plus, the environmental groups will never go for your plan," I tell him. "And neither will the people of Crest Lake. It will erode the beach. The Shoreline Liberation Front has made progress in other towns, getting blanket bans on structures and forcing people to move their homes back. They'll make your life miserable."

"I can handle them," he says. "I'm backing your plan. *Our* plan. Don't worry. Trust me, okay? I've got it all worked out."

I want to trust him. Really, I do. So, I try to picture a life with Doug after I leave this town. A comfortable life where we sit and talk and laugh. But all I can think about is taking Ryan down. I picture the look on his face when he realizes I've won, and a smile spreads across my face.

Doug brushes his hand across my cheek and pulls me in for a kiss. "That's my girl," he says. And we start on our dinner.

———

After Doug leaves, I get to work on my other project. Taking Ryan down. I followed him the other day. I took some photos and videos of him and some grungy-looking girl, and now I'm curating it. They were in a community college parking lot in Holland, making out in her car. I'm collecting evidence of his infidelity, and I wonder if he suspects anything about me and Doug.

I didn't feel emotional about it at all. I wasn't devastated. Ryan doesn't have that kind of hold over me anymore. The affair alone won't be enough to get him out of my life. If I confront him, he'll say it's my fault for letting myself go. That's a typical response of a narcissist. Blaming the other person. Making them think it's all their fault.

I cue up a video of a therapist who specializes in helping people leave toxic relationships with narcissists. The gaslighting starts early on, she says. It's a grooming process. At first, it's very subtle. It starts slowly, and it's peppered in with so much positivity that it's hardly noticeable. Just enough to get you to question yourself and your sanity.

*Check.*

Over time, they erode your self-confidence. Isolating the person from their social circle is another tactic. They'll badmouth your friends and relatives and try to get you to cut ties with them. Maybe even move you away, to isolate you even further.

*Check.*

My marriage, my entire relationship with Ryan, is literally a textbook narcissistic relationship, so I'm taking a clinical approach to combatting it. For example, I don't argue with

Ryan if he tries to tell me I'm wrong. If he says I was supposed to meet him at six, and I know we said seven, I don't argue. I'll say *that's not the way I remember it*, or *perhaps we're remembering it differently* because that doesn't leave room for escalation. I was hoping he might even get bored and end the relationship himself.

That's not happening, and it won't be enough to get Ryan to sell this house. He's adamant about keeping it. It's the last vestige of control he has over me, and it's going to take a lot more than a firm stance to get him to sign off on any sale. Of course, I could file for divorce. Get the courts to order him to sell. But people like Ryan don't take kindly to being left. They dig in. Make it ugly. Even resort to stalking or other dangerous behaviors. And it's not a marketable property now, anyway, so we're both stuck here.

*Together.*

Paging through the studies I've printed out, I get back to work, delving further into the pathology. As a consequence of caring about their image, narcissists have an Achilles heel: the capacity to feel shame. That's a big difference between a psychopath and a narcissist, and something that can work to help free me if I'm right about Ryan. If I can get something on my husband that shows who he actually is, and if I threaten to expose his awful behavior to the world, he may back down and give me what I want.

That is, unless I'm wrong, and he's actually a psychopath.

*In that case, he'll probably kill me.*

It's a gamble.

Then, I stumble upon something in one of the studies.

Narcissistic mortification.

*Death by embarrassment.*

Deep down, the author contends, narcissists are painfully insecure, so therapists need to be mindful of this during counseling, especially in couples therapy, and not push them too far.

*When a narcissist's view of themselves is challenged to the point where there's a disconnect between how they want to be perceived and how others are viewing them, it can destroy them. The fear of being humiliated or embarrassed consumes them. A sudden exposure of their true, ugly, imperfect selves can deal a crushing blow.*

For over a year now, I've been recording Ryan's outrageous behavior, curating clips, and filing them away. I was planning to use them in a divorce if needed. This gives me an idea. Suppose he doesn't agree to buy me out of the house and grant me a divorce. In that case, I'll threaten to unleash these recordings, exposing his despicable behavior to the world on every social media platform available. If he's a true narcissist, he'll do anything to stop me from doing it.

But if I'm wrong about him and he doesn't back down, I'll have to extract myself from the relationship immediately, leaving my nest egg behind. Because that would mean he's a psychopath, and it would be too dangerous to stay.

The study concludes with a warning. Suicidal ideation is more common among narcissists than most therapists realize, but the warning signs are absent. They show no outward signs of depression, so if they take that fatal path, it often comes out of the blue. At first glance, this makes no sense. Why would a person seemingly so full of themselves take their own life?

Because to them, the author explains, it's the ultimate way to take back control. A way to give the middle finger to the world or to saddle their partner with guilt and remorse. A way to have the final say and not let anyone dictate how their lives play out.

So, if I'm wrong about Ryan, if he's actually a psychopath, and I expose his behavior to the world, he might kill me.

*But if I'm right about him, he might kill himself.*

# CHAPTER 19
## KATE
PRESENT DAY

An incessant pounding startles me out of a sound sleep. It's coming from downstairs. I reach for my phone to look at the time. Who the hell would be banging on my door at eight in the morning? Margaret, maybe?

No. In all the years I've known her, she's only come by a handful of times and never dropped by so early in the morning. I whip off my nightshirt, throw on some yoga pants and a sweater, and head down, still in a daze.

*Why did I sleep so late?*

*And why am I so tired?*

Then I remember. I awoke last night, standing in front of my bedroom door, trying to pull it open. It must have been the wind that startled me out of my dream state. Something about fleeing a fire. The wind was loud and ferocious, whistling through the window that I'd left open a crack. Oddly, the sensation of cold air on my skin somehow morphed into a terrifying feeling of trying to flee an inferno that got my heart pounding. I couldn't get back to sleep for hours. Once downstairs, I peek out the window. It's Whittaker's car in my driveway.

*Great.*

I open the door. It's two of them this time.

"We've had some further developments," he says. "Can we come in? You know my partner, Sloane Davis."

"Yes," I say and let them in. "I just woke up. Can I get you some coffee?" I ask.

I notice that they're both holding takeout cups.

Whittaker shakes his head.

"I'm good," Detective Davis says.

"Well, I'm not. If I'm not under arrest, you'll have to wait for me to get some caffeine in my system. I'm sure it's some kind of constitutional right. And if it's not, it should be."

Whittaker smiles.

*A sense of humor.*

*Who knew?*

I usher them into the kitchen and they sit at my island countertop.

"Some ice water, maybe?" I offer.

They both accept.

"Did you watch the evening news last night?" Detective Davis asks.

"No. I came straight home and went to bed after the council meeting. Why? Is there something I should know?"

"The Mitchell's seawall was vandalized yesterday afternoon," Whittaker informs me.

My eyes widen. "What?"

"Here. Take a look," she says.

The detective pulls up some photos on her phone, and I page through them. A shudder runs through me as I take in the faux blood spatter and the chilling message.

"What time did this happen?" I ask.

"Around four in the afternoon," he says.

My chest tightens. This happened before anyone even knew that my plan was voted in last night. I wonder what they have in store for me now. At least the wall will come down, so they should be pleased about that.

"Do you think they'll come after me now? I'm sure they won't like my plan any better than that wall."

"They could. Which is why we wanted to warn you," she says.

"That's Daisy Parker's group. The Shoreline Liberation Front?" I ask.

"Yes," Whittaker says.

"But how does this all fit in with Gavin Mitchell and his arrest?" I'm so confused.

"We didn't arrest Gavin Mitchell. We brought him in for questioning. And we can't—"

I hold up my hand. "Yes, I know. You can't comment on an ongoing investigation. So, you came over here to tell me about the vandalism?"

"Not exactly," she says. "We have a few more questions for you based on something that came to light last night."

I walk over with my coffee and take a seat across from them.

"And?" I ask.

"Claudia Mitchell claims that you were having an affair with her husband," he says.

I've been expecting this, and I'm surprised it took them so long to find out. And I only have one move.

"Wait here," I say. "I need to get something for you."

I should have come clean about the affair earlier, and that's on me. I can still get ahead of this, though. My mind reels as I try to piece it all together. Gavin being detained. The vandalism. Could the Shoreline Liberation Front be responsible for Doug's murder? Daisy Parker, maybe? She's been on my property. Maybe she knew about Doug and me, and she's trying to screw with me and get him out of the way at the same time. Or was it one of the Mitchells? Punishing him for the affair?

All I know is that it wasn't me, so I race upstairs to get the burner phone and show them. It's proof that we were planning to double-cross Claudia and that I had everything to lose with his death and nothing to gain. I grab the shoebox from the top of the closet. It's . . . light. Too light. Nothing bounces against the sides as I pull it down off the shelf.

I fling off the lid, and my stomach sinks.

It's gone.

*Where the hell is my burner?*

There's no other proof about what we were planning. I have a quick look around, thinking maybe I took it out of the box in my sleep and misplaced it. It's not near the bed or my nightstand. Still, I need to get downstairs and tell them the truth.

*It'll be okay.*

Claudia surely has proof of our affair, and that would make her even more of a suspect, I'd imagine. Jealous wife murders cheating husband. It's surely enough for reasonable doubt. I wonder why she even told them about it.

I race back to the kitchen empty-handed. "You're not going to believe this," I tell them. "But it's the truth."

Starting from the beginning, I tell them everything. Our affair. How it started. How long it's been going on. My sleepwalking episodes. Our ruse to double-cross Claudia and leave for New York. The missing burner phone with the evidence.

"There must be some evidence of Doug's efforts to secure clients there. And his burner phone has to be somewhere," I say. "I had nothing to gain from Doug's death and everything to lose. Surely you can see that."

"Except for one thing," Detective Davis says.

"What's that?" I ask.

"Claudia Mitchell tells us that Doug was planning to break it off with you. Right before the vote," she reveals.

I swallow. I obviously underestimated Claudia. She knew about Doug and me, and she's trying to set me up. It's the perfect crime, really. Kill him. Throw the blame on me. Try to claim that he was going to double-cross me.

"Well, what else would you expect her to say? You're both smart people. Think about it. Her husband was cheating on her. *With me.* Isn't a spouse a more likely suspect in a situation like this?" As soon as the words leave my lips, I wish I could take them back.

Detective Davis narrows her eyes on me. "Yes, we always look at the spouse in the case of an unsolved suspicious death, don't we, Detective Whittaker?"

"We sure do," he says. "It's just good policing."

A wave of nausea washes over me, and bile rises in my throat—coffee on an empty stomach, coupled with a possible double murder charge.

"If I were you," he says, "I'd keep looking for that burner phone. And in the meantime, we'll follow up on your leads. If I were you, I'd do something about those sleepwalking episodes. That could be dangerous."

"We should be going now," she says. "If there's nothing more you want to tell us, that is."

"I've told you everything I know," I say.

Trying to steady my shaky hands, I escort them into the

living room and out my front door, almost dizzy with panic. I shut the door and lean back against it.

*I have to find that phone.*

There's another knock on the door.

*What now?*

I open the door.

*Margaret.*

I don't have time for this, but I invite her in.

"Sorry to stop by so early, but I was so worried when I saw what happened to the Mitchells. It's terrible, Kate. What's the world coming to? This used to be such a peaceful town," she says, wringing her hands.

And now I feel like a piece of crap. She's probably frightened to death, with a murderer on the loose, living all alone, and all I can think about is myself. She's the one person in this town who actually cares about me, and I need that right now.

"Come in," I say. "I'm fine."

I notice that she's lost a little weight, but I'm not sure if I should comment on it. You never know how an observation like that will land.

"What were they doing here?" she asks.

I'm not sure how much to tell her. The prudent move would be to call my attorney, but that's expensive. I'm not ready to confide in her about the affair, though.

"They had some questions about Doug's murder."

"I thought they arrested Gavin Mitchell," she says.

"They didn't arrest him. They detained him as a person of interest. And they don't seem too interested in him anymore. That's about all I know."

"Surely they're not thinking that you had anything to do with it?" she says.

"Well, we were in the middle of a feud," I say. "A very public one."

"You wouldn't kill him over the bluff," she says. "That's ludicrous."

I take a deep breath. "Margaret? If I tell you something, can you promise to keep it to yourself?"

"Of course, dear. I know I can be a gossip sometimes. But only about people who don't mean anything to me. Whatever you tell me, it's in the vault. You're like a daughter to me."

"Doug was on my side. He agreed with me that installing a seawall across the length of the bluff was a bad idea. He was presenting that plan to placate Claudia, but he didn't agree with it."

*Now, I have to lie a little.*

"We were hoping that I'd have enough votes without him. But if it came to that, he was going to throw it my way and deal with whatever fallout he got from her."

"Sounds like you and Doug were closer than I thought."

I shrug. "We were in agreement about the shoreline issue."

Margaret suspects something, I'm sure, but I'm not ready to disclose the affair.

"Well, do you have any proof of this?" she asks. "Because it would certainly put the spotlight back on Claudia if you did. I imagine she'd be hopping mad about that kind of a betrayal."

"I did. I had a burner phone. Doug did, too. But mine seems to have vanished."

"Vanished? Do you think someone broke in and took it?"

I hadn't even considered that. A shiver runs up my spine at the thought of it. Then I explain about the sleepwalking. She rests her warm hand on mine, which is freezing cold, as usual. It feels nice.

"The stress is getting to you, Kate. Maybe you should talk to someone. You're on your way to becoming a therapist yourself. You know that it could do you some good.

*She has a point.*

"I'll think about it," I say. "But there's more. Gavin voted my way last night. So my plan can move forward."

"That's fantastic!"

I shake my head. "I thought so too until—

Margaret's hand goes to her head. "The Mitchell's wall. Damn it. And now you're afraid they'll come after you. It's that same group, right? The Shoreline Liberation Front? The ones who threw the brick?"

"Yes."

What was that woman's name?"

"Daisy Parker."

"Didn't they arrest her?"

"Yes, but they dropped the charge to vandalism. I think she made a deal with them."

"What kind of deal?"

I have to confide in someone, or I'm going to burst at the seams. And Margaret's my only option, so I take a chance.

"She was sleeping with my husband. She told the detectives all about it. She claims they were in love, which is bullshit. And that he was going to leave me. She traded that evidence for leniency and tried to throw the spotlight back on me."

"I knew it," Margaret replies. "I'm so sorry, Kate. That little troublemaker will get what's coming to her; don't you worry about it."

"I'm not too sure about that. I know how it looks. They're convinced someone ran Ryan off the road that night, and now it looks even worse for me. Especially since I didn't come clean about the affair when it happened. And I have no real alibi, although my GPS confirmed I was in another part of town when it happened. But the timeline isn't perfect, and there's no evidence to prove for sure when he plunged off the cliff."

"Did you know about the affair?"

I take a deep breath. "Yes. I'd been following him. Getting photos and evidence. I confronted him that night. He said she meant nothing to him. Professed his love and all that crap."

"Oh, goodness. *Men!* Can't live with 'em and all that. You must have been devastated," she says.

"Actually, no. I was thrilled about it. Ryan was a bastard. I was hoping she'd take him off my hands. She'd be doing me a favor."

Margaret's eyes widen. "I see. In that case, why don't you tell me all about it? It'll make you feel better, dear. Tell me all about that bastard-dead husband of yours."

She's probably right, but I need to tread carefully.

So, I tell her some of it.

*But not all of it.*

# CHAPTER 20
## KATE


can't take living with him anymore. When he was ignoring me, I could handle it. But now Ryan's on the war path, trying to make me get off the shoreline committee. It seems that I'm an embarrassment to him, publicly disagreeing with his position that we should ban all structures and change the setback, forcing people to move their homes back.

Two nights ago, he grabbed my arm and squeezed so hard it left a bruise. Then he pushed me away from him so forcefully I stumbled and fell. This is new. He's never been physical with me before. He's escalating, and I need to take back control. Luckily, I installed a nanny cam that recorded all of it. I pretended to cower. I pretended I was afraid. Inside, though, I was seething.

Of course, after he blew up at me, he apologized. Tried to tell me it would never happen again. Said he'd make it all up to me. That's what they all say, and I know it's bullshit. But I accepted his apology and his dinner invitation.

*Because I have a plan.*

I know he's seeing that woman from his environmental group, and she'd probably be happy to take him off my hands. So I'm meeting him for dinner tonight, and I'm going to lay it all on him. He needs to move in with her, at least until we can secure the property and sell the house. Or buy me out and let me leave him. If he won't agree to it, I'll show him what I've got on him and threaten to unleash it to the world.

A narcissist would back down and give me what I want.

*A psychopath won't.*

It's risky, which is why I accepted his offer to meet for dinner. I need to do it in a public place. And if he doesn't react the way I expect him to. If he doesn't back down and give me what I want, it will mean I've misjudged him and he's actually a psychopath. And I'll have to leave, regardless of the financial consequences, because it will be too dangerous to stay.

So, I packed up everything that was valuable to me and loaded it in my car. I told him I wanted to meet him there like it was a date. Like we were starting over fresh. It made me sick to my stomach, the play-acting. I'm pretty sure I pulled it off.

———

We're at the only fine dining restaurant in town, if you could call it that. It's a steakhouse with linen tablecloths and a decent wine selection, but nothing like you'd find in New York or Chicago. We were planning on going to a waterside place in Saugatuck, but it's pouring rain, so we opted to stay closer. Dinner is going well so far. Mostly because I've given him everything he wanted. I wore the little black dress he likes on me, the sexy one that shows off my legs. I told him that I'd get off the shoreline committee. I said I wanted to start over, too—because I want to blindside him. Make him think he's won so that when I reveal what I have on him, it'll be all that much more of a shock.

"This is nice, babe," he says, reaching for my hand.

Those baby blue eyes. They make him look so innocent. Like a calm sea that beckons you to swim out further and then catches you in a rip tide, pulling you under until you're so far out at sea it swallows you whole. I've been beating myself up for letting him dupe me. But when he looks at me like this, I can almost dip my toe in again. I start to choke up, in spite of myself, thinking of how I felt about him when we first met and what my life could have been.

"Hey, what is it?" he asks.

"Nothing." I smile.

"Want another drink?" he asks.

We've each had one, so I decline. Ryan calls the waiter over and orders another one. I excuse myself and head to the restroom to run through it one more time before I lay it all on him. I don't need to use the bathroom. I just need a moment alone.

I smooth my hair in the mirror, stand up straight, and take a deep breath. A toilet flushes in one of the stalls. I take out my lipstick to freshen up a bit.

"Hello, Kate," a voice says.

My hand jerks as my head turns to the side.

*Claudia Mitchell.*

*Great.*

I grab a tissue and wipe away the peach streak I've left across my cheek.

"You're certainly jumpy tonight," she says. "Date night?"

"I didn't see you out there," I say.

"Doug and I just arrived."

"We're finishing up."

"Too bad. We could have joined you. That last dinner we had a while back was so much fun." Her snarky tone lingers in the air between us as she washes her hands, and I finish touching up my lipstick.

"They say timing is everything," I say.

When I exit, I see Doug sitting across the room, but I don't make eye contact. Instead, I head right for the table and tell Ryan it's time to head home in a breathy tone and a sly look on my face that belies my true intentions.

He smiles, downs his drink in a few big gulps, and pays the tab.

---

It's not ideal to have this conversation with the rain beating down on us and Ryan holding an umbrella over our heads. Hopefully, the downpour will muffle the sound a bit. Since this is the only place in town to dine, there are bound to be other people we know within earshot, and I don't want anyone to hear what I have to say.

He opens my car door, holding the umbrella over my head. "I'll see you at home, babe," he says, and he goes in for a kiss. "Can't wait."

I pull away and hold up my hand. "No, Ryan. You won't."

His face seems to go pale, if that's even possible, to see in this light, as if the blood has drained from his head.

"Kate? What're you . . ."

"I know about your little fling, Ryan. I have proof, so

don't try to deny it. You can go stay with her. I want a divorce," I say. "And you're going to give it to me."

He smiles now. He thinks it's cute, I can tell. Flattering even. "You're jealous? Of her? Look, Kate. She means nothing to me. It was a mistake. She threw herself at me, and I was weak. I'll break it off with her, I swear. Right now. I love you, Kate. Only you. Forever."

My face hardens. By the look on his face, he's pretty shocked. "No, Ryan. I'm not jealous. I'm done. I want a divorce, and I want you out of the house. I can't stand living with you for another minute. Move in with her. We'll sell the house. Or you can buy me out. Whatever, but I'm not wasting another day of my life with you."

His face changes before my eyes. It's subtle. A seething, calm-before-the-storm look. One I've seen before.

*Set jaw.*

*Clenched teeth.*

*Flared nostrils.*

"That's never going to happen, and you know it," he says in a low rumble.

I'm scared out of my mind, and I'm starting to tremble. The look is positively terrifying. I stand my ground and narrow my eyes on him. "Oh, yes, it is. I've been recording you, Ryan. In all of your ugliness. All the times you've belittled me. Mocked me. Hurt me. And I'm going to release it all to the world if you don't give me what I want."

He smirks. "You're bluffing, Kate," he says. "You don't have it in you."

"Try me," I say. "Call my bluff. Then see what happens."

He doesn't flinch. I've wiped the smirk off his face, but it's replaced with a terrifying blankness. My recently eaten meal turns in my stomach as the fear grips me. My heart races, and

I'm on the verge of a full-blown panic attack, but I steady myself and hold his gaze.

His blue eyes are like ice now. Cold. Calculating. He's not afraid.

*But I am.*

I play a clip for him. The altercation from the other night, his face twisted like a gargoyle, hardly recognizable as he rips into me, grabs me, and shoves me down.

"There's more where that came from. So go home. Pack your bags. Go to your girlfriend's house before you don't have that option anymore because I just recorded you saying she means nothing to you. If you don't, I swear, I'll ruin you. I'll give you two hours. Be gone when I get home. Or else."

He drops the umbrella, grabs my hand, and squeezes it around the phone as he pulls me into him. The edges dig into the sides of my hand, but I take the pain as we lock eyes.

He pulls me into him. "Stop this now!" he says, his face inches from mine, his hot breath a stark contrast with his ice-cold stare.

"I have copies everywhere, Ryan. I'm not stupid." I pull my hand away. "Now go!" My arm flies up, and I point to his car. He's not cowering, though, and I wonder if I've over-played my hand.

"This isn't over, Kate," he says. "It'll never be over."

He marches off into the stormy black night, leaving me dripping wet and terrified. I'm trembling as I tuck myself into my car, take a deep breath, and try to decide what to do if he doesn't comply with my demand. I stare at the phone, thinking about the clip I showed him and all the other ones I've squirreled away.

*Are the cards I'm holding in my hand the ticket to my freedom?*

*Or are they a death sentence?*

If I'm right about him, he'll leave tonight. But if I'm not, and he doesn't. What then?

Do I use what I have? Because if I actually send all of this out and he is a psychopath, he'll have nothing to lose.

*And I'm sure he'll kill me.*

I start up my car and follow him as he leaves the parking lot, at a total loss about what to do next.

# CHAPTER 21
## TRAVIS
PRESENT DAY

"It seems unlikely to me that Kate Breslow would make up a story about having a burner phone and then pretend to lose it," Chief Thompson says.

"That's what we thought, too," Sloane says. "But we wanted to run it past you. See if it struck you the same way."

Chief called as they were leaving Kate Breslow's house, directing them to stop over at the station. Immediately. Travis and Sloane briefed him on the case, which is growing more complicated by the hour.

"I have some news, too," Thompson says. "Now that the Shoreline Liberation Front has escalated their tactics, C-GIS is coming out. They want our full cooperation," Chief says, looking squarely at Travis. "You get that?"

*Coast Guard Investigative Services.*

Travis has been expecting this, but he doesn't have to like it. The Coast Guard's involvement will only complicate the investigation. He stands by his assessment of Luke Jenkins and his merry band of paint splashers. They're not murderers. He'd stake his career on that. And whoever killed Doug

Mitchell could probably give a rat's ass about the shoreline. It was more personal, he's sure of it. But a directive is a directive, and he'll play along.

"I get it," Travis says. "Our full cooperation."

He tells Chief Thompson his take on Jenkins, along with his gut feeling that the murder of Doug Mitchell is something more personal than environmental ideology.

"Anything else, Chief?" Sloane asks.

"Nothing on my end," he says.

"We're waiting on a warrant. So we can get that member list from Jenkins," Travis informs him.

"I'll call over and see what I can do," Chief offers.

"Now that they've escalated their tactics, it should be a priority," Sloane adds.

"I hope you're right about this, Whittaker," Chief says. "They might not be as harmless as you think. So, keep an open mind. Both of you."

———

"Are you going to tell me what she meant?" Sloane asks Travis.

They're in the bullpen of the precinct, trying to diagram out everything they know about the case. Doug Mitchell was having an affair with Kate Breslow. Any of the Mitchells could be upset about that. Claudia Mitchell claims that her husband was going to dump Kate Breslow, and Breslow could be bitter about that. Then there's Daisy Parker, who has it in for Kate Breslow and who has already vandalized her home once. And then there's the Shoreline Liberation Front, Luke Jenkins, and the rest of them.

"Travis?" Sloane repeats. "I asked you a question."

"What who meant?"

"Margaret Brenner," she says. "You said you'd tell me later." She offers up her hands. "It's later."

They ran into Margaret Brenner when they headed to their cars after interviewing Kate Breslow at her home earlier this morning. Margaret asked them to back off Kate and take another look at Daisy Parker.

"It's nothing," Travis says. But he knows Sloane won't let it go.

"She said she'd done you a favor years ago. And now you could do her one by treating Kate better. What was she talking about?" she asks.

"It's stupid high school stuff," Travis says. "Will you let it go? Please? We have a homicide to solve. And the Feds are going to be up our asses pretty soon. We need to make some progress while we still have control of the case."

She lets out a huff but doesn't press it. "So, what's our next step? Want to take another run at Luke Jenkins?"

"Yeah. And Daisy Parker. We need that warrant," Travis says. "Divide and conquer?"

"Sure. What's your pleasure?" Sloane asks.

"I'd like your read on Luke Jenkins," he says.

"Let me call the chief. See if he's made any progress on that warrant," Sloane replies. "We need that list. Any of them could be going rogue. I'll try to get it over to Jenkins today."

———

The morning flew by. Travis barely had time for a stop at the restroom, never mind lunch, so he's delighted that Sloane has come back with some sandwiches from a local deli. It's after two already, and he's starved.

She plops one in front of him. "Pastrami," she says. "Although you'd be better off with turkey."

"Thanks."

She likes to nag him about his eating habits. He finds it endearing. Ripping open the paper packaging, he grabs the sandwich and digs in, taking a hearty bite. A morsel gets stuck in his beard, and he thinks again about shaving it off.

"I got the list from him," Sloane says. "There were eight people at the meeting, in addition to Jenkins and Daisy Parker, the day Doug Mitchell was killed."

"We've got bigger problems," Travis says, washing down his mouthful of pastrami with a sip of lukewarm office coffee. "Daisy Parker seems to have disappeared."

"Disappeared? As in . . ."

"As in, she's nowhere to be found."

"Has someone filed a missing person's report?"

"No. Not yet. Too early. And I don't think anyone would miss her enough to do that. Her boss said she didn't show up for work two days in a row. She's not answering her cell. It goes straight to voicemail. I went by her apartment. Nobody's seen her for days. And she wasn't with the shoreline group when they vandalized the seawall."

"Maybe she went on a trip," Sloane offers.

"Without getting time off from work?" Travis shakes his head. "Her boss said she's reliable. Not the type to skip out. I asked the boss to file a report if she doesn't show up soon. There's nobody else to do it. I'm not holding my breath, though. She didn't seem too interested in the whereabouts of Daisy Parker."

"What do you think it means?" she asks.

"Maybe nothing. Maybe something. Too early to tell."

"We need to get more video footage. Anything we can

find in the area on the day of Doug Mitchell's death. Check it against all of their license plates. Kate Breslow, the Mitchells, Parker, Jenkins. This timeline isn't foolproof. Somebody was somewhere they shouldn't have been that day. And we're going to find out who it was."

# CHAPTER 22
## KATE

After Margaret left, I tore my room apart, looking for that damn burner phone. I didn't leave the room last night, as far as I know, so I didn't bother searching the rest of the house. But then, how do I know for sure? I could be sleepwalking every night, wandering around the house like a zombie.

It's unlikely that I would open the door and lock it again, but not impossible. People have even driven cars while sleep-walking. Maybe I should set up the nanny cam and record myself overnight. At least I'll have more of an idea of how bad it is. Therapy is not a bad idea, but it's not a priority for me at the moment.

Margaret wants to give me the money to consult with an attorney, but I don't feel right about taking it from her. I'm not as destitute as I let on. Not yet, anyway. I still have a small amount of money in another account. One that Ryan didn't know about. Enough for my portion of the shoreline revital-ization and a little extra for my move. She's probably worse off than I am.

In the meantime, I'm putting my plan into action. I've decided that I need to get out of here as fast as I can. Since the vote went my way, I'm meeting with the contractor who will do the work on the bluff. He said it should take about three months, but I don't have to stay here while it's being completed. As soon as I get it underway, I can put my house on the market and go.

My clinical externship can be completed from anywhere. I only have another year left and I'll be able to practice as a Doctor of Psychology. It pays much better than a child life specialist, but in the meantime, back in New York, I can scrape by doing my old job.

Then I think back on what Margaret said about the phone before I mentioned my sleepwalking. She asked if someone might have broken in the house and took it. I've had that feeling several times in the last few days. The feeling that someone's here, watching me. In moments of weakness, in the darkness of night, I picture him.

*Ryan's ghost.*

Haunting me from beyond.

*It'll never be over, Kate,* he said that night. In the parking lot of the steakhouse, as we stood in the pouring rain, when he crushed my hand with that look on his face that made me shudder. He wanted to kill me, that much I know. But I don't know if he would have actually done it.

*But he never got the chance.*

Because, as it turned out, that was the last night of his life. That's the night he and his Jeep went careening off the winding road that meanders up to our bluff, shattering into a thousand pieces on the rocks below, ending my nightmare, or so I thought. I know that ghosts aren't real, but he's in my head. All the time. Maybe that's what he meant. It'll never be over because he'll be haunting my psyche.

*Forever.*

Then I think about what Margaret said about the keypad. And the fact that Daisy Parker was probably in my house with Ryan. She could have seen him punch in the number. Maybe he even gave it to her.

*Could she have come in and taken the burner phone?*

*Could she be trying to drive me mad?*

I need to go on the offensive and find her. She blames me for taking Ryan away from her. If I show her that clip of him saying she means nothing to him, along with how he treated me, she might see him for what he really is and back off.

It's risky to go looking for her, but I need to try.

———

"Is Daisy Parker working today?" I ask.

I'm starting with her workplace, which is about half an hour away. The coffee shop in Chikaming where she was working last year, although I have no idea if she still works here. It's got a rustic vibe with picnic bench-type booths and a handful of two-tops scattered around that look like they're made of wine barrels. The store manager is a middle-aged woman with shoulder-length brown hair, a hearty build, and farm-girl hands, dressed in jeans and a thick sweater. She's not too happy about the interruption.

"Popular girl," she says, as she wipes the counter and then throws down a dishtowel. "You're the second person to come looking for her today. A detective from Crest Lake was here about two hours ago. No, she hasn't shown up for work all this week. He asked me to file a missing person's report. Like

I have that kind of time on my hands." She motions to the chaos.

*My stomach sinks.*

It had to be Whittaker, which means that this was a very bad idea. I need to get out of here. I might have been the last person to have seen her last night in the parking lot, and that's not good.

"Oh, I see. Is that . . . unusual for her?"

She barks at an employee. "We need more milk. Go get some from the back. Hurry!" A young man nods and scurries into the back and out of view. She turns back to me, her hands on her hips. "And you are?" she asks.

"I . . . um. I'm a friend. I couldn't reach her, so I stopped in."

She narrows her eyes on me, her hands on her hips. "I've never seen you around town. Are you from around here?"

My heart starts racing. "You know, I need to get going. I'll stop by her apartment."

She looks me up and down. "You look like a lady of leisure, and I'm a busy woman. You should call that detective from Crest Lake. If you're her friend, then you can file the report. Wait here, and I'll get his card so you can let him know."

My chest tightens, and I feel like I'm not getting enough air. Daisy's missing, and now I've mixed myself up in it. I bolt out the door, race to my car, and curse myself for being so impetuous.

*Where the hell did she go?*

*Why did she disappear?*

*What's my next move?*

# CHAPTER 23
## KATE

*he enemy of my enemy is my friend*—I hope.

My engine idles as I sit in the driver's seat, second-guessing myself. I don't know if anyone's home. They keep their cars in the garage, and the front door is shut. I get out of the car, ring the doorbell, and hold my breath.

After a few minutes, a flood of relief washes over me. This was a bad idea. I turn and make a run for my car, grateful that I have an out. Then, the sound of a car rolling over gravel fills my ears, and I hear the garage door rise.

*I'm too late.*

Claudia Mitchell locks eyes with me as she pulls into the driveway behind me, blocking me in where my car sits in front of their open garage. She could have pulled her car into the other side. Instead, she leaves hers behind me, turns off her car, swings open the door, and jumps out, not even bothering to close it.

"What the hell are you doing here?" she barks.

"Claudia, we need to talk," I offer.

Her hands are on her hips now. "What would I possibly have to talk to you about?"

"I think we're both in danger," I say. "I heard what happened to your wall last night. It's the same group that threw a brick through my window. And Daisy Parker accosted me last night. In the parking lot, before I went in for the vote. I think we need to put our differences aside."

She takes a step towards me. "Why on earth would I do that?"

"Because I think Daisy Parker's behind this. She's out to get me. Out to get all of us. But me, in particular."

Claudia takes a moment to study me, her arms folded in front of her. "Why you, in particular?"

"Because she was sleeping with my husband," I say.

"*Your* husband? Then what were her underpants doing on *my* husband's boat?"

My eyes widen. "What?"

She lets out a huff. "You didn't know. Damn it, Kate! I shouldn't have said anything. You're trying to pump me for information again."

"I'm not, Claudia. I swear. I came to warn you. I went looking for Daisy Parker today. And I found out she's missing. The police have been looking for her, too. I think she went underground. She might be plotting something. Please hear me out."

"I don't see what you could possibly—"

"Give me ten minutes. *Please.*"

Claudia lets out a long sigh. "Ten minutes. But that's it," she says.

She marches back to her car, grabs her purse, and slams the car door, leaving me blocked in. My wheels turn as we walk to the house in silence.

*Did Daisy Parker seduce Doug and kill him to get back at me?*

*Is she that much of a nut job?*

"Where's Gavin?" I ask. "He should hear this, too."

"At work," she says.

We get settled in the living room, Claudia on the sofa and me on a wingback chair across from her. I take a deep breath and try to steady my nerves.

"First, I want to tell you something. And say that I'm sorry. I was having an affair with Doug, which I think you already know. It was wrong. And I regret it. I want to try to explain to you where I was coming from."

"I don't want your excuses, Kate."

"It's not an excuse. It's an explanation," I offer.

She rolls her eyes.

"I went looking for Daisy Parker this morning to show her something, but now I'm going to show you," I say.

"Sure. Whatever."

"My husband wasn't the man he pretended to be. I thought if I could make Daisy see how horrible Ryan was to me, that she'd somehow back off of me."

"I don't see how this has anything to do with—"

"Please. Give me my ten minutes."

She looks at her watch. "Eight minutes."

"When I first met Ryan, he swept me off my feet. I barely knew him when we moved out here. At first, it was magical, but once I was isolated and alone, he started to change. Gaslighting me. Eroding my self-esteem. It was subtle at first. Then, it escalated to the point where I'd lost myself. This happened a few days before his car accident."

I play the clip, and Claudia shrinks back from the phone with a look of horror on her face. But she catches herself, and her face hardens. "I still don't see what this has to do with me."

"I was weak and vulnerable when I met Doug. He showed me kindness, and he helped me reclaim my sense of self-worth. I misinterpreted that as love, and it was a mistake. A fantasy. A way out of my private hell."

"Why Doug, Kate?" she asks.

"I didn't plan it. It just . . . happened," I say. "We were working together on the committee. One thing led to another."

"I saw the way he looked at you that night when the two of you came to dinner. Ryan wasn't fooling everyone. I could see that there was something off about your husband. But instead of coming to me, woman to woman, you tried to take my husband from me."

"Claudia, I'm sorry. But you weren't exactly welcoming me with open arms. I was lonely. In New York, I had friends. A job."

"What about your family? Why didn't you go to them?"

I give her the short answer.

*There's nobody left.*

She pries, so I add some details.

"I lost my mother to cancer when I was six. Then my father was killed on nine-eleven. I had my grandmother, but she died right before I met Ryan. I was an easy mark for a guy like him."

She looks away and then back at me. Her lip starts to quiver like she might break down. I sense it's not out of compassion or empathy, though.

"I had my suspicions about the two of you," she says. "And I confronted Doug that morning. The day he died." Her eyes start to tear, her voice breaking as she struggles to hold it together. "And you know what he said? He said you needed him. And I didn't."

Her tears erupt into a full-blown sob. I excuse myself to get a tissue from the bathroom and let her cry it out. Things are going better than I expected, but I'm guessing we're still not at a hugging-it-out kind of place. I hand her the tissue upon my return. Her sobs have slowed to a trickle.

She pats her eyes and takes a deep breath. "He needed to feel like the strong one, and you gave him what I couldn't. But I'm not as strong as I seem. I had to be when my first husband died. I had two little boys to raise. Doug liked playing the part of superhero. I'm used to being in control, though. It makes me feel secure. Then I got so stubborn about this house. It's my home. It's been in the family for genera- tions. This view, this yard. It's all I've ever known. But I let it come between Doug and me. And that was wrong. If I could have a second chance . . ."

"I'm so very sorry, Claudia. I didn't love him like that. I'm sure what he felt for me was simply infatuation. It was a fantasy. It wasn't real. What you had with him? That was real."

She looks off in the distance, talking as much to herself as to me. "The day he died, he said he would break it off with you. But he wasn't changing his mind about the shoreline. He was still planning to back you. I was angry, and we ended on a sour note. If only I could do it all over again. Tell him how much I love him. I didn't know it was the last time I'd ever see him."

"He knew, Claudia. I'm sure he knew."

In terms of their relationship, I'm not sure if Doug changed his mind about me or if he was just telling her what she wanted to hear, but that part doesn't matter to me anymore. He didn't change his mind about the shoreline revitalization plan, and I need to get her to admit that to the detectives.

I need to tread lightly here, though, because I'm on thin ice with her as it is. She's given me exactly what I need to throw the spotlight off of me and onto Daisy Parker, though, and I need to use it to help clear myself.

"Well, at least you know that he wanted to make the marriage work. He was angry with you, Claudia. But that didn't mean he didn't love you anymore. In my experience, the opposite of love isn't anger; it's indifference. If he still cared enough to have a blow-up about it, then there was still a spark there."

She nods, and her face grows softer. Not quite a smile, but almost. I want to ask her about Doug's burner phone. I don't want to push it, though. Did she find it? Or is it somewhere in this house? Where did those phones go? I need something to corroborate what I told the detectives about Doug and me and our plan to double-cross her.

"You said he wasn't changing his mind about the shoreline committee," I say.

"Yes. He said it was the right move."

"Claudia. Did you tell the detectives that?"

She looks away, fiddling with a strand of hair. "I don't think I'm supposed to talk to you about that."

"You know it's a crime to withhold information from the police. This is a murder investigation, and we all want to catch who's behind this. I'm telling you, there's something wrong with that Daisy Parker woman. And on this, we need to present a united front."

"What are you suggesting?"

"Let's go talk to the detectives together. Try to get to the bottom of this before someone else gets hurt. Tell them every-thing you told me."

She rolls her eyes again. "I suppose that's the prudent move."

"Great."

"Listen. Kate. I'm sorry about Ryan and what you went through. And that I wasn't more . . . accessible. I'm sure you felt very alone. But that doesn't excuse the fact that you slept with my husband, and we'll never be friends."

"I respect that, Claudia."

"Now, let's get down to the station before that lunatic strikes again," she says.

The enemy of my enemy isn't my friend.

But for now, she's my ally.

*And that's good enough.*

# CHAPTER 24
## TRAVIS

"Y ou've got visitors," the front desk officer says over the precinct phone line. Travis heads to the lobby to see Claudia and Gavin Mitchell with Kate Breslow, looking like a mob of angry villagers, minus the pitchforks.

He gets them settled in an interview room, wishing that Sloane wasn't at the ME's office over in Kalamazoo. It's three-on-one right now, and he could use an ally.

"The gang's all here. To what do I owe the pleasure?" Travis asks.

"We're concerned about the disappearance of Daisy Parker," Kate Breslow says.

"How do you know about that?" Travis asks.

"I went looking for her today," Kate Breslow says. "And her boss told me she hasn't shown up for work for a few days. She told me that you were looking for her, too. Daisy accosted me last night. Right before the vote."

Gavin Mitchell jumps in. "You didn't think to warn us?

The woman's got a radical streak. She was on Kate's property, two homes down from us. She's a member of the group that vandalized our seawall. Why don't you start doing your damn job and protect the people of this town instead of trying to turn this into something it isn't?"

*Here come the pitchforks.*

"Calm down, Counselor. We have our protocols, and she's not missing. Officially. Nobody's even filed a report, and that wouldn't be in our jurisdiction anyway." He turns to Kate. "So why didn't you report this altercation? You could be the last person to have seen her."

"Cut the bullshit," Gavin says. "Stop throwing it back on us. We're all persons of interest to you, and in your tunnel vision state, you're leaving us exposed."

"Well, you're in luck. A special agent from C-GIS is coming in from Detroit any minute now to take over the investigation."

"C-GIS?" Kate asks.

"Coast Guard Investigative Services," Gavin says, turning to Kate. "C-G-I-S. C-GIS, for short. They have jurisdiction over the shoreline and certain maritime crimes."

"Is that why you're here?" Travis asks. "To lay into me about Daisy Parker? Or do you have something to tell me?" He turns to Kate, going on the offensive. "What made you go looking for her in the first place?"

"I wanted to talk to her about Ryan. She's angry with me because of him, so I thought if I could make her see who he really was, she'd back off of me."

"Tell me about this confrontation last night," Travis says.

"Daisy came at me in the parking lot of the town center. Out of nowhere, as I was heading in. She warned me to back off my proposal. And she said she was sure I'd done some-thing to Ryan. And that if I didn't cooperate, I'd regret it. She grabbed my arm rather forcefully and got in my face."

"It didn't occur to you to report this?" Travis asks.

"I guess it slipped my mind with everything else that happened at the meeting." She turns to Gavin. "It only lasted a few minutes. That's why I went to see her again today. To try to reason with her. To show her who Ryan really was. He was fooling her like he'd fooled me."

"And who was your husband? Really?" Travis sits back now, folds his arms, and tries his best not to look impatient.

"He was a cold-hearted narcissistic bastard, and I can prove it," Kate says. "Have a look at this."

She pulls out her phone and plays a video. In the clip, Ryan Breslow's in a rage, ripping into her about the shoreline issue. He gets physical with his wife, throwing her down on the ground, and Travis can't help but wonder why she'd risk showing this to him. It seems like even more of a motive for murder, and her husband's death is still an open case.

Maybe she's laying the groundwork for a battered wife defense. Or she's trying to get him to lay off her out of compassion. He has to admit he does feel a bit more sympa-thetic. Wife-beaters deserve the death penalty, as far as he's concerned. The law is the law, though, and he's bound to uphold it.

"I wanted her to hear this, too," Kate says. "I recorded it the night of his accident. We were out at dinner. Ryan wanted to patch things up, but I confronted him about Daisy in the parking lot."

She plays a recording of someone, ostensibly her husband, saying that Daisy Parker means nothing to him and that he'd break it off with her.

"You see, I wasn't a jealous wife," Kate says. "I would have been happy for Daisy to take him off my hands. Maybe Ryan broke it off with her that night, and she didn't take it well. Does she have an alibi? Did you even check into that?"

"What does this have to do with the Mitchells?" Travis asks. "Why are they here with you?"

"Because I went to see Claudia today. To apologize. And to explain where I was coming from when I got romantically involved with her husband. You see, when Doug and I got on the shoreline committee together, I was vulnerable. I made a terrible mistake. We had an affair, but it didn't mean anything. I've apologized to Claudia for that indiscretion. I'm not sure if she'll ever forgive me, but we've decided to put aside our differences for the time being because we're both afraid of what might happen next if you don't start looking seriously at Daisy Parker."

"Travis," Claudia breaks in. "I told you that I confronted Doug that day about his affair. And that he told me he was planning to break it off with Kate. But I didn't tell you that Doug also told me he was going to back Kate's plan. Like my son told you, it seems as if I was the last holdout on the shoreline issue, and I'll never forgive myself for getting into an argument with my husband over it that night. I can be stubborn. But for Christ's sake, I didn't kill him over it. So, as my son said, do your job and find this Daisy Parker woman before she comes after one of us. Facts are facts, and the fact is that her DNA was found on the boat, not ours."

Claudia Mitchell makes a good point. Daisy Parker on the boat still makes no sense, though, unless Doug Mitchell was a dog who was also sleeping with Parker, which Travis doubts. And Parker was in love with Ryan Breslow. That much is pretty clear.

"You should have told us that earlier," Travis says.

"I'm telling you now, and surely you can see I have nothing to gain from that admission. So, find my husband's killer. Before someone else gets hurt," Claudia says.

Could he be wrong about Luke Jenkins? Could Jenkins be a psychopath, a Charles Manson type? A charismatic mastermind who convinces vulnerable young women to do his dirty work? During the interview, Jenkins tensed up when Travis mentioned Ryan Breslow. Was Jenkins jealous of Breslow? Had Ryan Breslow challenged him for the spotlight? Or for Daisy's affection?

Travis needs to find a way to bring in Jenkins. Make him take a polygraph. If he's a psychopath, he might be able to beat it. But still, it would give them another chance to assess the guy. In the meantime, he'll get the Feds working background on Jenkins. Now, he's anxious to get rid of them and collaborate with Sloane.

"Thank you all for coming in. This is all very helpful."

He appeases them as he wraps things up and ushers them out of the precinct, but he's still not convinced of anything at this point. Maybe Kate Breslow and Claudia Mitchell made a black widow pact. With their cheating husbands gone, they're both the sole owners of some very valuable lakefront property—no messy divorces to get in the way and dilute their net worth.

*Stranger things have happened.*

Everything's on the table, and Travis is anxious to get the results of the tox screen, which Sloane is bringing back from the ME's office. This is all connected, somehow. So he steps back and looks at the bigger picture, trying to see the pattern. But all he sees are a bunch of dots, leading him around in circles, making his head spin.

His desk phone rings, and he picks it up.

"Whittaker? Special agent Jesse Carver from C-GIS is here to see you."

"Send her in," he says.

*Things are about to get a lot more interesting.*

# CHAPTER 25
## TRAVIS

"Jess," Travis says. "It's been a while."

She's dressed in black slacks, a white blouse, and low-heeled pumps. Her dark, shoulder-length hair is a bit shorter than he remembers. The elegant lines etched on her face somehow enhance it, evidence of a hard-won wisdom that he finds alluring. Standing in the doorway of the conference room for a few long moments, they keep their distance from each other. Neither a handshake nor a hug seems quite right.

"How've you been?" she asks.

"We've got a complicated case on our hands," Travis says. "Why don't you take a seat, and we'll get to work."

She nods, then looks down at the floor. Travis motions to the spot across from him. They both sit, and he starts to take her through it. He's about halfway through bringing Jesse up to speed when Sloane enters the conference room.

"I'm Special Agent Jesse Carver," she says, standing up to greet Sloane.

"Detective Sloane Davis. Nice to have your help on this."

The two of them shake, and Sloane fills them in on the latest from the ME's office.

"Doug Mitchell's official cause of death was drowning, but he had Estazolam in his system," Sloane reports. "It's a benzo, normally used as a sleep aid, but sometimes used for anxiety. Not enough to kill him, but enough to knock him out. About three times the normal dose. And about a drink's worth of alcohol on an empty stomach."

"If his official cause of death was drowning," Jesse asks, "any chance this was an accident? Someone wanted to drug him and have him miss the meeting? But then he fell overboard? Or maybe there was some kind of scuffle?"

"Anything's possible," Sloane says.

They run through the suspect list. With federal resources, they'll be able to get background on Luke Jenkins, Daisy Parker, and the other members of the Shoreline Liberation Front more quickly. They decide to divide up the responsibilities, with Jesse taking the Shoreline gang and Sloane and Travis staying on the locals.

"You were starting to fill me in on your interview with Luke Jenkins," Jesse says to Travis. "What's your take on him?"

"Seemed to me like an armchair activist. That's why I pushed him a little," Travis says, explaining how he goaded Jenkins, implying that he was soft. "I'm not sure if that's what prompted him to pull the stunt with the Mitchell's wall. But if it did, it confirms that he's got an ego. He doesn't like to be challenged."

"I got the same vibe about the ego," Sloane says. "Called himself 'Professor Jenkins.' Probably enjoys having students fawn all over him."

"Is he attractive?" Jesse asks.

"I'll let Sloane take that," Travis says. "He's not exactly my type."

Jesse smiles.

*It lights up the room.*

"I suppose," Sloane says. "In a bookish sort of way. More like charismatic. He's a zealot about the environment, and I could see the students flocking to him. No official reports of any misconduct on the job, though."

Travis fills the two women in on Luke Jenkins and his reaction at the mention of Ryan Breslow's name.

"Do you think there was some kind of rivalry there?" Jesse asks.

"Could be," he says. "Maybe he killed Doug Mitchell and framed Daisy in retaliation. But let's assume Ryan Breslow's death isn't related for the moment. Stay on Doug Mitchell. What do we know?'

"We're looking for someone with access to benzos who wanted Doug Mitchell to miss that meeting," Jesse says. "So, I'll go through the member list from the Shoreline Liberation Front and narrow it down. Who else might have wanted him to miss the vote?"

"It depends on what and who you believe," Sloane says. "Claudia Mitchell admits that she and her husband were at odds over the vote. Seems unlikely that she would divulge that information if she murdered him. But then, you never know. Cheating spouse. Jealous wife. That's the least complicated explanation."

"But we've also got Gavin on the boat," Travis says. "Claiming he went there to talk his stepfather out of his plan. Maybe he was angry about the affair. The betrayal of his mother and all that. Maybe the story about him backing Kate Breslow's shoreline plan was a smokescreen."

"But you said he had an alibi for the time Doug Mitchell was out on the lake," Jesse says, resting her chin on her thumb and index finger.

"He does. He still could have been the one to slip him the drugs, though," Travis says. "While it was on the dock."

"How did the boat get back to the dock if nobody else was on it?"

Sloane makes a good point.

Somebody had to be on the boat with Doug Mitchell.

"And we've got Daisy Parker's underpants on the boat," Jesse says. "Maybe Daisy seduced him. She would have wanted Doug Mitchell to miss the meeting. But you two don't seem to think that's likely."

"We need to find out who had access to Estazolam," Travis says.

"Wait," Sloane says. "It's a sleep aid. Kate Breslow sleepwalks." She grabs her computer and punches the keys in a rapid, staccato motion.

"Kate Breslow sleepwalks? How did that even come up?" Jesse asks.

Travis fills Jesse in on Kate's missing burner phone and the fact that Kate offered the sleepwalking as an explanation for why it disappeared.

"Bingo." Sloane's hands fly up from the keyboard. "Estalozam's used to treat sleepwalking."

"And she would have a motive to frame Daisy Parker," Travis says. "I always thought Kate Breslow was hiding something. There are too many coincidences for her hands to be clean. Maybe Doug broke it off with her, like Claudia said, right before the vote, and she didn't take it well."

"That would have taken some planning," Jesse points out.

"Drugging him to miss the vote and framing Daisy Parker doesn't sound like a spur-of-the-moment decision."

"We have to start somewhere. But we can't get her medical records without a warrant," Sloane says. "We don't have enough for that. This is all speculation."

"You said Ryan Breslow was involved with the Shoreline Liberation Front. Right?" Jesse asks.

"We think so, yes," Travis says. "Luke Jenkins confirmed that Breslow went to a few meetings with Daisy Parker."

"Let me work on this from the federal level," Jesse offers. "Domestic terrorism investigation. Gives me a reason to search the homes of all of them, including Kate Breslow, if her husband was mixed up with them. You can find a reason to search the Mitchell's home again, given the results of the tox screen. It might take a week or so to get the paperwork lined up, but if we keep quiet about what we found and surprise all of them, at least it gives us a chance to look for the drug. That might be enough for an arrest in the event we find something. Even if we don't find the prescription, we might find something else."

"And none of them will see it coming," Travis says.

*Least of all, Kate Breslow.*

# CHAPTER 26
## KATE

Walking to the edge of the bluff with my morning coffee, I take in the view of the giant CAT excavator digging into the shoreline below and the boulders they cart down each morning, strategically placing them to form a bulwark against the erosion. The rumbling of the heavy equipment on the shoreline below me gives me hope, a stark contrast with the nagging feeling in the pit of my stomach that something awful could happen at any minute.

I turn and head inside. The wind has picked up again, and it's almost as loud as the construction noise, although at a higher pitch. I won't miss that when I'm gone. It's been nearly a week since we met with Whittaker, and there's been no word from either of the detectives. Nothing about the case. Or Daisy Parker. Or Doug's cause of death. Rather than dwell on the past, though, I'm choosing to move forward.

A real estate agent is on her way over to look at my property and prepare a listing proposal. It's not the best time to sell with interest rates so high, but I have to try. If worse comes to worst, I could always rent it out. I've got a few feelers out for internships starting in January back in New York. It's October already, and I didn't realize how hard it would be to line something up. I should have gotten on that earlier.

I set up a nanny cam in my room, and I've not had another sleepwalking episode since the night I lost my burner phone, which is good and bad. Good, because it means I'm not putting myself in danger. But bad, because I still have no explanation for where that phone went.

I've torn apart my bedroom, and it's not there. It has to be somewhere, and I suppose the best I can hope for is that I wandered around the house with it in my sleep and left it somewhere. I'd like to find it myself rather than leave it for a future owner. Nobody could get in here without my new alarm system going off, so if someone came in, it had to be before the alarm was installed. I make a mental note to tell the agent about my new state-of-the-art system, which will certainly be a selling point.

There's a knock at the door, and I greet Vicky Perkins, the top listing agent for Van Buren County, specializing in lake-front property. A fifty-something woman with shoulder-length blonde hair, dressed to the nines in a sharp red suit over a crisp, white blouse, looking like she just stepped out of a brochure. She's well established, with clients both here and in Chicago and other big cities looking for their piece of paradise.

"Come in," I say.

I offer her some coffee, but she declines, and we begin a tour of my home. Starting with the backyard, I launch into a lengthy discussion of the shoreline renovation. I show her where my property line will end once they re-angle the bluff, and I discuss the plan to revegetate it, which will slow the erosion.

She points to the heavy equipment down below and then over towards the remaining pile of boulders still sitting in the corner of my yard, waiting to be taken down the steep switchback pathway they dug out of the bluff's clay foundation. "It would be better to put the house on the market after the work's been completed," she says, stating the obvious. "Do you perhaps want to wait a few months?"

I smile politely. "If I wanted to wait, I wouldn't have brought you here today." I hope she gets my drift and doesn't push it any further. I don't owe her any explanations, and if she wants my business, she'll be smart about this and move on.

"Noted," she says. "It's my fiduciary duty to inform you, that's all."

We proceed with a tour of the ground floor interior. She's impressed with the quality of my home, and I feel proud of myself. The house is comfortable and inviting, yet classy and elegant. I mention the recent security upgrades, and she stops in her tracks.

"Did something happen? To prompt that upgrade? I know there've been some threats, and I saw on the news about the Mitchell's wall. If there's anything of that nature, it would need to go in the seller's disclosure statement."

My stomach sinks. I hadn't thought of that. I explain to her about the brick being tossed through my window, and I tell her the perpetrator's been arrested and charged.

*I leave out the part that she's now missing.*

"That's unfortunate," she says. "Especially since the same group went after your neighbor. Perhaps now that there's a concrete plan to fix the shoreline moving forward, we could spin it in a way that won't do too much damage." She eyes me and adds, "As long as there are no further incidents," letting me know she expects to be kept in the loop.

We head upstairs, first to the master suite and then to the two guest bedrooms. As we're entering the smaller one, something jumps out at me. There's a slight, almost imperceptible divot in the comforter, as if someone's sat down on it, got up again, and tried to smooth it back out but didn't do a very good job. I try to remember the last time I was in this room. Probably over a month ago. Did I sit on the bed for some reason? I don't remember doing so, but I suppose I could have.

While the real estate agent's checking out the closet space, something catches my eye under the nightstand. It's shiny and black. I reach under and grab it.

*My burner phone.*

*How in the hell did it get here?*

She turns around in time to see me stand up.

"Oh, I've been looking for this," I say, slipping it into my pants pocket so she doesn't catch the fact that it's an old-school flip phone. I don't need her asking any more questions. Thankfully, it's not something she dwells on, and now that we've finished the tour, she's pretty much giving me her sales pitch. I'm only half-listening as we wrap up our conversation, and I see her downstairs and toward the front door.

"I'll get you comps and a proposal by tomorrow, midday," she says.

"Thanks, Vicky," I say, and I usher her out the door.

Closing it behind me, I grab my phone out of my pants pocket and flip it open. The battery's dead, so I rush upstairs to find the charger and plug it in, trying to stay calm. In all probability, nobody was in my home. Why would someone take the phone from my room and then leave it for me to find in the guest room?

The last time I looked at the burner was after my first sleepwalking incident when I awoke on the edge of the bluff. So, this means I must have unbolted this door, wandered out of my room, reentered it, and bolted it shut again. It's become a rote action. A bedtime ritual, like brushing my teeth, which I've also done while sleepwalking as a kid.

*But why would I go in the guest room, of all places?*

That makes no sense, but I suppose it doesn't need to. Dreams don't make sense, so why should sleepwalking? It's dangerous, wandering around in the middle of the night in a trance, but at least now I won't be able to exit the house without the blaring alarm waking me.

I purchased a bed alarm, but I haven't hooked it up yet. I've been reluctant to use it because it can wake me when I toss and turn or get up to use the bathroom in the middle of the night. Now that I think I might have unbolted my bedroom door in my sleep, I may need to rethink that. Putting my sleepwalking concerns aside for the time being, I focus on the bigger threat, which is contributing to my overall stress—and the sleepwalking.

*Where is Daisy Parker?*

*Is she planning to come after me?*

———

A pounding on my door startles me.

*"Open up!*

*Federal agents!"*

I look out my window, and I'm seized with a fear so visceral that my knees go weak. I have to crouch down because I feel like I might pass out. It's just after lunch, and the chicken salad I ate turns in my stomach. A wave of nausea hits me, and I feel as if I might throw up. Trying not to hyperventilate, I slow my breath. Steadying myself against the wall, I make my way to the door and open it.

"C-GIS special agent, Jesse Carver. We have a warrant to search the premises," the woman says, holding up a badge. I've never seen her before. The look on her face is serious but kind, and I'm actually relieved it's not Whittaker. I wonder if this means that the Coast Guard has taken control of the case.

*Why would they be interested in me?*

"Come in," I say. "What's this about?"

She hands me a sheet of paper.

"You can read the warrant," she says. "Please take a seat and get comfortable. This might take a while."

"I have the right to call my attorney?" I ask.

"Yes, ma'am. That's your right," she replies. "Now, please. Have a seat." She motions to my living room.

A half-dozen agents divvy up the work in an orderly fashion. One stays with me, posted like a sentry next to the sofa where I sit, trying to steady my shaking hands so I can read the warrant. It explains that they have good cause to search my home as part of a domestic terrorism investigation.

*Domestic terrorism?*

*What could that possibly have to do with me?*

This sends me into a complete panic. I recall this from 9/11. Anything related to terrorism gives the government broad powers to investigate and severely curtails civil liberties via the Patriot Act. Some of those provisions have expired, but some were made permanent. I have no idea what my rights are, and I suddenly regret not being a more engaged citizen. She said I could call my attorney, so I do.

After that, all I can do is sit and wait. And wonder.

*Is this another fishing expedition?*

*Or will I be hauled off in handcuffs?*

Then I remember the burner phone. It must be fully charged by now. Surely, that will work in my favor. They'll see that Doug and I were planning to dupe Claudia. This will throw the spotlight back on her. Rather than waiting for my attorney to arrive, I decide I should tell them about it before they find it. I don't want them to think I was hiding it from them.

I turn to the agent guarding me. "Can you get the special agent?"

"Agent Carver?" he asks.

"Yes. The woman who served me the warrant. I found my burner phone this morning. I'd misplaced it, but today I found it. In my guest room. I need to show her what's on it."

After a few minutes, Agent Carver comes to me with the burner in her hand. "Ms. Breslow. Is this the phone you were referring to?"

I swallow, hoping that I'm not making a grave mistake. They always tell you to say nothing to the police without an attorney present. I have a gut feeling that this is the right way to play it, though, so I take a chance.

"Yes."

"And you have something to show me?"

"I do," I say.

She sits beside me. I open the phone and locate the text streams. The exchanges that, hopefully, will clear me for Doug's murder and stop them from digging any further into my personal life.

I take a deep breath and hope for the best.

# CHAPTER 27
## TRAVIS

"Jesse's on her way over," Travis says to Sloane.

"Is she bringing the burner phone?

"Hope so," he says.

While Jesse and her team searched the Breslow home yesterday and investigated the Shoreline members, Travis and Sloane served warrants on Claudia and Gavin Mitchell yesterday morning and came up empty-handed on the pharmaceuticals. The family had its share of medications on hand, but none of them matched the tox screen.

Which makes sense. If one of them had drugged Doug Mitchell, they would have been smart enough to get rid of the evidence. They were hoping to find something else of value, but nothing useful had turned up.

He found Claudia home alone. She was still sleeping at her son's place, but she'd stopped home to pick up some of her belongings. Her demeanor was different without her son around. She seemed skittish to him like she had something to hide. He wishes that Sloane had been there with him, offering her interpretation of Claudia's behavior. That was his way of checking himself. A way to avoid confirmation bias. Nobody is right all the time, and he values his partner's opinion.

Gavin's place needed to be searched at the same time to capitalize on the element of surprise, and Sloane took the lead on that search. Gavin reportedly made a few threats about malicious prosecution and a harassment suit. He repeatedly stated that he'd come forward, admitting that he was on the boat. Sloane reminded him that he hadn't. That it was the video footage that had placed him on the boat and forced him to come clean. In the end, Gavin cooperated and let them do their jobs.

"Claudia seemed more nervous this time," Travis says.

"Nervous, like she had something to hide? Or like she wasn't sure what to say without her son present?" Sloane asks.

"Not sure," Travis says. "What about Gavin's disposition?"

"He was angrier this time," she says. "It seemed genuine, but then my radar's not infallible."

Genuine anger usually meant innocence.

*Feigned anger meant guilt.*

"Gavin and Claudia both profited from Doug's death," Travis says.

"True. It's the most logical explanation, too," she says.

"Except for Daisy Parker. How does she fit into this?" he asks.

"Maybe Claudia somehow knew about Ryan Breslow's affair with Parker. She planted the panties to make it look like Kate tried to frame Daisy," Sloane offers.

"She'd have to be some kind of criminal mastermind,"

Travis says. "That's a lot of layers. How long has she even known about the affair? Breslow's car crash was over a year ago. And how would she get access to Daisy's thong?"

"I'm anxious to see that burner phone. Maybe it'll give us a clue."

Yesterday, during the search, Kate Breslow told Jesse that she'd found her burner phone earlier that morning when she was showing her home to a real estate agent. At least the warrant had turned up something useful, even if it corroborated Breslow's claims that she and Doug were planning to dupe Claudia. It also put the spotlight back on Claudia and Gavin Mitchell; neither of them had any proof of what they'd told the detectives.

A call comes in, alerting him to the fact that Jesse's arrived.

"Send her in," he says.

Jesse strides into the conference room. Travis feels a little flutter, but he does his best to shut it down. So far, Sloane hasn't seemed to pick up on the fact that there's some history between the two of them, and he'd like to keep it that way. It was over a decade ago. She's been married for nearly ten years.

*Hard to believe.*

They've already checked in with each other about the drug search and the fact that they'd all come up empty-handed on that.

Jesse and Sloane greet each other.

"Hey, Travis," Jesse says.

"Hi, Jesse," he says.

They hold each other's gaze for a moment too long. Sloane shoots Travis a curious look.

"Did you bring the burner phone?" Travis asks.

Jesse shakes her head. "No. They're still working on it. I have a transcript, though. I've got some important news on Daisy Parker. She left her computer behind. We found it in the dumpster at her apartment complex. Wiped clean. We were able to restore her search history and recover some files. I just got the report from our tech team. Seems like she was obsessed with Kate Breslow."

"Obsessed? How so?" Sloane asks.

"She'd been researching her. Following her. Had all kinds of photos of her. Of Kate and her husband. Kate and Doug Mitchell, boarding his boat. And Kate with some older woman. Her mother, maybe?" Jesse asks.

"No," Travis says. "Her mother died a long time ago." His mind flashes to Margaret Brenner, who seems to be pretty chummy with Kate.

"So, Daisy Parker's been near the Sundancer," Sloane says. "That's certainly interesting."

The three of them sit around the conference table, discussing what this might mean. Daisy knew that Kate was having an affair with Doug Mitchell. So maybe to get back at Kate, she seduced Doug and killed him. If she was careless enough to leave her computer in the dumpster, she could have forgotten her underwear on his boat.

"She's got quite a record, too," Jesse reports. "Drug problems. Petty theft, as a teenager. A few fistfights. I was able to peek into the sealed files. And a TRO from a guy she dated a while ago when she was living in Wisconsin. I touched base with him briefly. It seems like she's the jealous type. From what I can tell, she didn't take it well when he broke it off with her. She even approached his eight-year-old daughter in the park one day after he wouldn't return her phone calls, demanding that the girl tell him who her father was seeing. That did it for him. After he filed the TRO, she backed off."

"A restraining order," Travis says. "Well, that fits with how she's been acting towards Kate Breslow."

"What about Luke Jenkins?" Sloane asks. "Anything there? Any evidence that he and Daisy were involved? Or that he put her up to killing Doug Mitchell?"

"He denies everything," Jesse says. "But then, you never know. He's got a squeaky-clean record. Not even a traffic ticket in the last five years. Claims he has no idea where Daisy Parker is. He claims she started to change after Ryan Breslow's death. She grew increasingly more erratic and unreliable. The group didn't sanction her throwing a brick through Kate Breslow's window, and he wanted to make that clear. He suspects she may have started using drugs again, although he has no proof of that."

"We need to put an APB out on Parker," Travis says. "She's the key to all of this. Do you think you have enough?" he asks Jesse.

"I'll make it work—domestic terrorism investigation. Gives me wide latitude," Jesse says with a smile.

"You have that phone transcript?" Sloane asks.

"Yep. Here you go." Jesse places it on the table.

Sloane pages through it. "It seems to corroborate everything Kate Breslow told us. Doug Mitchell was planning to vote her way and then ask Claudia for a divorce after the meeting that night."

"But let me show you something," Jesse says, reaching for the transcript. "On the next page." She turns to the exchange and rests a slender finger on the line of text. "Right here." She taps the paper. "Kate texts Doug about two hours before the meeting. There's no response. After six minutes, she texts him a second time, asking if everything's okay."

"Interesting," Travis says. "Can I see that?"

Jesse passes the paperwork to him.

"If our tech team can verify that Kate sent this text from her home, then we know she wasn't on the boat with him," Jesse says. "In effect, this clears her for Doug's murder."

"It also means that Claudia Mitchell could have been telling the truth," Sloane says. "Doug could have changed his mind about the divorce after she confronted him that morning. Seems like it was unusual for him not to answer Kate right away if she texted him again after only six minutes. Maybe he didn't know how to tell her he'd changed his mind."

"Or . . ." Jesse says, looking over at Travis.

"Or maybe he was already dead," Travis says.

Jesse nods.

Sloane lets out a sigh. "So, we're nowhere, really. No closer to figuring out who did this, aside from eliminating Kate Breslow."

"Let me get to work on that APB," Jesse says. "I'll see myself out, and we can touch base later. You better warn Kate Breslow, though. If Daisy Parker's as unhinged as we think she is, she might be in danger."

Travis nods. "Will do, Jess."

As soon as Jesse's out of earshot, Sloane turns to him. "Spill it, Travis. What's up with you and Jesse Carver?"

He rolls his eyes. "Later," he says. "After I pay Kate Breslow a visit."

"Travis!" she calls out as he races to the conference room door. "You can't leave me hanging like that."

*But that's exactly what he does.*

———

"Detective Whittaker," Kate Breslow says. "What happened to the C-GIS agent?"

"She's got her hands full. Local guy like me? I've got all the time in the world."

"Do you have a warrant for my arrest this time? Or do you want to have another look around?" she asks.

"No, actually. I came to apologize," he says.

Her brows rise. "About?"

"And to warn you. May I . . . come in?" He's still on the other side of her screen door. They've always been awkward around each other, and he can't put his finger on what it is about her that he finds so unsettling.

She lets out a sigh and opens the door for him.

Travis steps inside.

"Make yourself at home." She motions to the living room area, and the two of them sit, she on the sofa and he on her side, in an armchair.

He plants his feet on the ground and leans in, resting his hands on his legs. "We have an APB out on Daisy Parker. An all-points bulletin," he says. "And a warrant for her arrest."

"Why? Do you think she murdered Doug?"

"I can't really comment on that. It seems like she was obsessed with you, though," Travis says. "We searched her apartment. She had photos of you. Lots of them. Of you alone. You and Ryan. You and Doug. She's been following you. And after the incident with the brick and her accosting you at the town council meeting, I wanted to warn you. She may very well have left town, but you never know. I would suggest filing for a TRO. A temporary restraining order."

"I see," she says flatly, and he can't say he blames her.

He's been a bit of an asshole to her this past year or so. "Thanks for letting me know."

"Of course," he says.

"I'm putting my house on the market. I'll be moving back to New York soon," she tells him. "I assume I'm free to leave town."

Travis is still suspicious about what happened to her husband. Maybe she had something to do with it. Maybe she didn't. But since he's seen proof that Ryan Breslow was a sadistic abuser, he has less of an interest in pulling on that thread. At least he's got an explanation for her muted demeanor, and it adds up. Domestic abuse will do that to a person. Some women never recover, and he hopes she can move on and heal. She's got a core of inner strength, he senses, and that will serve her well. And he's not going to look any further into her involvement in Ryan Breslow's death.

The couple was out to dinner the night he went careening through the guardrail to his death. The night she claims that her husband was trying to patch things up. And based on this new information, it's quite possible that Daisy Parker was stalking them. Maybe Parker saw the two of them in an intimate moment at the steakhouse and lost it. Followed her lover and ran him off the road. It's certainly possible, if not probable, given her history.

"Yes, Ms. Breslow. You're free to do as you wish. And I wish you luck wherever you end up."

"Thanks," she says.

"Do you have anywhere else you can stay until you leave for New York?"

"I've installed a state-of-the-art alarm system. I've got a panic button next to my bed. I'll be fine," she says.

"Still. I'd advise you to check into that restraining order against Daisy Parker. At least it would allow us to take action in the event she approaches you again."

His phone rings, saving him from an awkward exit.

"I need to take this," he says. "I'll see myself out."

# CHAPTER 28

# TRAVIS

"Okay, you're back. And you owe me an explanation," Sloane says as Travis enters the conference room.

"A deal's a deal," Travis says. "What do you want to know? You want all the juicy details or just the broad strokes? I could tell you stories that would make you blush, Sloane. This one time, we were over in Detroit, working a case. Jesse came out of the bathroom wearing this—"

"Please! No." Sloane covers her ears.

Travis laughs.

"I'm just messing with you," she says. "You don't need to tell me anything you don't want to. But I'm here. As a friend, if you need to talk. Seems like she was . . . special."

Sloane means well, but her tender smile borders on pity, and it makes Travis feel weak. That's a very uncomfortable feeling for him, so he shuts it down.

He shrugs. "She was. I appreciate your offer. But I'm good. She meant something to me once, but that was a long time ago. She's married now. Two kids."

Sloane nods, and he's glad she doesn't push it.

The truth is, he's not very good at relationships. Jesse was the closest he'd ever come to making a real commitment, and he didn't blame her one bit for dumping him and moving on, although it took the wind out of him for a long while when she did. He can't blame his failed relationships on his parents. Or his childhood. Or that one true love that got away. It's just the way he is.

It's not a sex thing. It's not like he needs the variety or the excitement of bachelorhood. He likes being with one woman. But the thought of sharing his private space. His private thoughts. Every waking moment of his life, with someone. *Anyone.* It's never appealed to him.

He'd have been happy to keep things the way they were with Jesse indefinitely. Long distance but monogamous. That wasn't enough for her. It's not enough for most women. She moved on, and that was that.

"How's Kate Breslow doing?" Sloane asks.

"She seems okay. Planning to put her house on the market and move back to New York."

"Seems about right," Sloane says.

"So where are we on the Doug Mitchell case?" Travis asks.

"I'm combing through that new video footage we got from near the dock, the day he went overboard. Maybe we missed something. Can you take a look? You're much more likely to recognize someone from around here than I am. I saw Gavin Mitchell walk towards the boat area and come back about twenty minutes later. That's about it."

Travis has deep roots in the area, and Sloane's a relative newcomer, originally from a suburb of Detroit, although she lives in Grand Haven now. She's getting herself up to speed, but there's no substitute for the lifetime of memories he has to draw upon.

"Sure. Let me have a go at it. How's married life, by the way? Since this seems to be a day of sharing," Travis says.

"It's not much different from cohabitating life," she replies. "Aside from the awesome gifts, of course." She gives her head a smug shake. "It's good. You might want to give it a try someday."

Travis rolls his eyes. "Why don't you go pick us up some lunch and let me concentrate?"

"It's only ten o'clock. All I'm saying is. Don't knock it till you've tried it."

He shoots her a look.

"Lunch it is," she says.

———

The footage from the camera near the dock is at a weird angle. It doesn't show the actual boats, only the people walking to and from the parking lot to their slips. The authorities have already confirmed that there were no suspicious individuals around that morning that they noticed. All were boat owners, aside from Gavin Mitchell.

Travis has been at this for over two hours, and he's almost cross-eyed. You'd think with cameras perched on practically every street corner and home these days, they'd be able to catch every criminal in the act and get them to confess right there in the interrogation room.

In reality, it doesn't work like that. It takes an enormous amount of concentration to watch grainy video, frame after frame, hoping to find one specific piece of useful evidence.

Plus, most camera feeds have limited storage. Unless the feed is backed up somewhere, which is rare, the footage will be taped over in a few weeks, at most, so they have a short window of opportunity to find anything of use.

Even if they do find something or spot someone on tape, it's hard to get a positive ID from a video that will hold up under cross-examination. If it doesn't prompt a confession or convince a suspect to take a plea deal, it's not very useful. But it's his only hope, so he stretches his aching neck, rolls his shoulders, and keeps at it.

He's working in the conference room, not out in the bullpen of the precinct, but it's not soundproof. One glance towards an errant sound. One weak moment of spacing out and checking his phone, and those few frames might whisk by unnoticed, concealing the perpetrator and the crime. It's not a fun job. It's tedious and backbreaking.

After what seems like forever, Sloane returns and plops a wrapped-up sandwich next to his computer. He unwraps it, in need of a break.

Turkey.

*Great.*

"What did I do to deserve this?" he asks.

She smiles. "Your heart will thank me.

He rolls his eyes.

"Anything of interest on the tapes?" she asks.

"Might be. I spotted two people with homes on the bluff who had a stake in the outcome of the vote that night. One of them is Sam Bolger, the council president. The other is a woman named Noreen Garfield. Then there's another woman whose name escapes me. She was pretty vocal in the effort to ban vacation rentals, which was also being voted on that night. The Mitchells are pro-vacation rental. They all have boats at this marina, so they have reason to be there. We've already questioned Sam Bolger. We might try taking a stab at the other two."

"Should we divvy it up?" Sloane asks.

"Sure," Travis replies.

"What we really need is to catch a break on the other end," Sloane points out. "At the Saugatuck dock. None of the people you spotted have a reason to be there. Why don't I take a drive and see if I can find any other cameras in the vicinity, even in another part of town? If we can catch someone anywhere in Saugatuck, even away from the dock, at least it would put them in the area."

"Good idea," he says.

"Maybe wait on questioning them? See if I can find something first. We don't want to tip anyone off."

Travis nods. "In the meantime, I'll check in with Jesse. See if she's got anything of interest."

"Yeah, you will." Sloane winks.

He shakes his head. "Just go, Slone."

———

"I told you. The answer is no!" Jesse is borderline shouting into her cell phone as she charges into the conference room. "Let me talk to your father," she says.

Her hair is in a ponytail today, and she looks adorable. Like a spunky soccer mom. The kind you don't want to mess with—sporting a firearm. She cups her hand over the phone and talks softly, but her furrowed brow reveals that it's something serious.

Travis imagines some kind of family drama. The kind that will blow over, like you see on a sitcom. The kind they'll all laugh about later. Jesse married someone outside law enforcement. A tax attorney. A nice-looking, clean-cut guy who bought her a very big diamond and likely remembers their anniversary every year, unlike some other guys.

"Sorry," she says as she slides the phone into her pants pocket. "Co-parenting issues."

He brings her up to speed on the video footage and Sloane's reconnaissance mission to Saugatuck. As he does, he starts to imagine what their home life is like. Then he realizes that he's anxious for her to leave. He doesn't need this kind of complication clouding his powers of analysis and knocking him off balance.

"I've found nothing to indicate that Jenkins or any of the Shoreline Liberation Front members were anywhere near either of those harbors on the day of Doug Mitchell's murder," she says.

"Let's try something else," he says. "Let's see if we can find any evidence of who may have had access to Daisy Parker's apartment. We need to find out how that thong got on his boat."

Jesse nods, and they run through the various possibilities for what feels like the one-millionth time. As they're spinning the evidence, a thought pops into his head.

*Co-parenting issues.*

*Isn't that what divorced people say?*

He glances at her left hand; it's still sporting what looks like a two-carat diamond ring and a plain wedding band.

"Travis?" she says. "Are you listening to me?"

"Sorry, Jess. I'm burned out from combing through the footage. I need some coffee."

"I asked for the transcripts from the neighborhood board meetings and the public hearings. I'll go through them again.

See if anything jumps out that we can connect to any of the people you saw on the dock that day."

"Sure," he says.

He hands her the folder and heads out to get a coffee he doesn't really want. And now he's even more anxious to close this case and get on with his life.

# CHAPTER 29
## KATE

A lot can change in twenty-four hours.

After Whittaker left, in effect telling me I'd been cleared of any suspicion for Doug's murder, I got a call from an attorney representing some entity. I forget the name. Sounded like one of those shell companies that people make up when they want to remain anonymous. LTL Enterprises, or something like that. Somehow, word got out that I was looking to put my house on the market.

This attorney supposedly has an all-cash offer for me, a little under-market price. It sounds a little fishy, but then what do I care? I've been given the green light to leave town, and I'd like to take advantage of this window of opportunity. With Daisy Parker lurking in the shadows and my name cleared for the time being, it's in my best interest to go as soon as possible. Nothing is holding me here.

I pull my Prius into a parking space in Crest Haven. I asked to meet at a public place, given the fact that someone might be trying to kill me. This could very well be a ruse to get me alone, so I wasn't about to meet at my house or the woman's office. She invited me for coffee, and we're meeting at a small upscale café with a partial view of the lake that used to be a bed-and-breakfast. It's quaint, like an English country cottage, with a white picket fence and pretty purple violas housed in tidy rows of flower boxes under the windows.

I enter The Coffee Cottage and look for a brunette wearing black slacks and a peach blouse. It's mid-morning and not very busy. A woman holds up her hand and smiles. The smell of roasted coffee beans complements the savory scent of butter, making my mouth water.

I walk over. She stands and holds out her hand. "Sarah Williams," she says.

"Kate Breslow," I say.

We shake, and then we both take our seats. So far, she looks harmless, but my guard is up. The waiter arrives and I order a latte. She's already been served; she's sipping what appears to be black coffee. A blue folder sits next to her napkin.

She gets down to business. "I have an all-cash offer," she says. "And it's take it or leave it. My client isn't going to negotiate on the price."

"Noted," I say, not really liking the sound of that. "I suppose you can't tell me anything about this mystery buyer."

"No, I can't."

My head spins with the possibilities. Is it some drug lord trying to launder money? A rich family looking for a getaway? Again, why do I care? If the price is right, I'll take the deal. My mind flashes back to the conversation I had with the listing estate agent who toured my home. She said that I'd have to disclose that Daisy threw a brick through my window. And I've been warned that she might come after me again. *And she's missing.* This offer could be a godsend. Thankfully, I didn't sign an agreement with the agent yet, so I'm free to sell. I don't want to appear too eager, though, so I try to put on a poker face.

"How did you find out I was considering selling? I haven't put it on the market yet."

She smiles politely and shrugs.

"Right," I say. "You can't tell me."

"It's not important," she says.

My latte arrives, steam rising off the brim. I blow on it and take a cautious sip.

Her eyes trace my hand's movement, and then she looks up at me. "My client's impressed with your shoreline plan. Nice job getting that pushed through, by the way. It seems as if the work will be completed quickly. Just in time, right?"

"What do you mean?"

"I'm speaking in geological time, of course. The shoreline was a ticking time bomb. You never know what could happen. Another season like the one we had in eighty-six and many of those homes on your bluff could be lost forever."

She's referring to 1986 when a severe storm season resulted in catastrophic flooding in multiple states and the collapse of dozens of homes along Lake Michigan.

"See that beach right out there, Kate?"

"Yes," I say.

"Looks inviting, no?"

I shrug. "Sure, I guess. I'm not much of a beach-goer."

"In 1938, a tsunami came out of nowhere. Killed ten people. Technically, it was a meteotsunami," she says. "They're caused by storm systems, not earthquakes. The lifeguards tried to warn everyone that the weather might turn, but you know how people can be."

I remember Doug telling me something about that.

*Don't they have warning systems in place for that sort of thing now?*

*And why is she harping on something that happened nearly a century ago?*

"My client's impressed with the fact that you've gotten your plan approved, against all odds, to secure the homes on the bluff. Considers it a reflection of your work ethic. And that work ethic, it's assumed, also went into the renovation of your home. I'll need to do an inspection, though, if you decide to take our offer. There will be no agents involved, which means no commissions to pay. So even an under-market offer will provide you with a substantial net gain."

"I'll need to have my attorney review the paperwork," I say. "*If* I take the deal."

"Of course," she says.

She takes a sip of her coffee, dabs her lips with her napkin, and places it on the table.

"So, let's cut to the chase, Sarah. Give me a number," I say, both pleased with and surprised by my boldness.

She takes out a pen, writes a number on the lipstick-stained napkin, and pushes it over towards me.

My eyes widen.

*A pretty big number.*

I do the mental math. It's more than I thought it would be and pretty close to what I would get for a full-price offer, minus the commission. This gives me pause. It seems too good to be true.

*Does she know something I don't know?*

I've got a bird in the hand, though, and I don't have to

sign anything this minute. I can still back out after I have my attorney look at the paperwork and have had time to do some research.

"Let's set up that inspection," I say.

"Wonderful. How about three pm tomorrow?"

"Sure," I reply.

"I need to go now," she says. "Look this over in the meantime."

She taps a manicured finger on the blue folder, stands up, and leaves.

As I take in the view of the lake, I realize I need to decide where exactly I'm headed. Sooner rather than later. Somewhere with a view of the water, maybe. I've gotten quite fond of it.

Not a lake.

*Maybe a river.*

————

The rest of my day was glorious. The best one I've had in ages. Because I finally figured out my next steps. I grew up in New Jersey, across the Hudson from New York, in a town called Demarest. I don't want to move back there, but it got me thinking. Manhattan doesn't feel right to me, but neither does a suburb in Jersey. So, I started to research some of the towns on the other side of the Hudson, in Westchester. One that's close to the train line, where I could easily pop into the city. There are so many. And lots of new development along the waterfront. I've gotten attached to the water view, and it would be hard to give up. I'll need to go visit to pick the right town, but I'm committed to the general plan.

I've secured two externships. One is at a large, prestigious hospital in Manhattan, and the other is at a smaller psychiatric center in Westchester, in a village called Katonah, a lovely little town with cute shops and restaurants. I used to go on day trips there when I lived in the area. Although it's better for my career to intern in the city, I've decided to go the other way. The smaller facility is interested in having me work with their child and adolescent population, and that's a good fit for me. Working there two days a week, I can finish the externship in about six months. In the meantime, I can contract with local hospitals as a child life specialist.

*This feels right.*

A new start. In a somewhat familiar place.

My phone buzzes, and I'm hoping it's not the attorney, Sarah Williams, calling to tell me the deal's off. It's Margaret, not Sarah. I let it go to voicemail, and a pang of guilt needles me. I send Margaret a text stating that I can't talk at the moment, but I ask her to have lunch with me later in the week. After the inspection. When I know for sure that I'm leaving.

Telling her in person is the right thing to do. If we talk on the phone, she might pick up on the fact that I'm hiding something. She texts me back, telling me she's busy every day except Friday, and that makes me feel better.

*If she's busy, she'll be fine without me.*

We confirm our Friday lunch. Then, a text comes in from Vicky, the listing agent, asking if I've made a decision. I text her back, stalling, telling her I'm still mulling it over. After the inspection tomorrow afternoon, I'll tell her I've gone another way.

*Hopefully.*

I get to work finding a real estate attorney. The offer sounds good to me, but I need some guidance on this. I find someone suitable, call the office, and line up an appointment. Once that's done, I get back to the exciting part. Researching all the cute little towns on the Hudson with easy access to the city. I'd like something walkable, with shops and restaurants, a good place for singles. I don't want to count my chickens, though, so I won't start looking at houses yet. Everything's going great.

*And I don't want to tempt fate.*

# CHAPTER 30
## KATE

The inspection went well, and the final paperwork arrived today for the house sale, three days after I met with the mystery buyer's attorney. I'm on my way home from my meeting with the real estate attorney who's representing me on the transaction. After reviewing the deal, I signed off on it. The mystery buyer agreed to let me rent back until the end of November so I can finalize my move, but the proceeds should be in my account tomorrow or the day after.

Even without paying a commission, the net proceeds will be slightly less than I might have gotten if I'd put it on the market, but then you never know. The Shoreline Liberation Front seems to have mellowed a bit due to the federal investigation, but a buyer could still be spooked by the potential for trouble down the road. Plus, with all the media focus on climate change and eroding shorelines, it's better to sell this place sooner rather than later. Cash is cash, and I'm itching to get it in my hands.

As I pull into my driveway, my mind wanders back to the

first time we came to see the house over six years ago. So full of hope for my new adventure.

*So in love.*

A sadness washes over me as I think of how differently my life could be right now if Ryan wasn't who he turned out to be. Would we have started a family? Would this home be filled with the delightful chaos of toddler tantrums? Sticky high chairs? Toys scattered across the living room? I picture myself nagging Ryan about the mess. He apologizes, and those crystal blue eyes pierce my armor. We hug, and one thing leads to another.

*The mess can wait, babe,* he says.

A normal marriage with all of its ups and downs. All of its imperfections but all of its little joys. But I remind myself. That would never have been my reality. And I picture the look in his eyes that last night. The night I told him about the evidence I'd collected.

*Pure rage.*

Would he have turned that on his own children, or would that have been reserved for me? And how can I ever trust a man again?

*How can I trust myself?*

Not bothering to pull into the garage, I park the car in the driveway and head for the front door. I punch in the key code and open it. The alarm system beeps, and I start to step inside to head for the control panel. Then my body tenses and the hairs on the back of my neck stand up.

Someone's behind me.

I turn around.

*A gun is pointed at my head.*

"Turn off the alarm, Kate. Nice and easy. Or I'll blow your brains out."

I freeze for a moment as terror rips through me.

Then, I force myself to comply.

*Quickly.*

Because I believe her, I'm sure she'll kill me if that alarm starts blaring.

"Okay, Daisy. Whatever you say."

She follows me in as I head for the keypad and disarm the alarm. My hands are trembling, but I steady them long enough to punch in the numbers. All the while, I see the barrel of the gun in my peripheral vision, aimed at my temple.

"What do you—"

"Shut up, Kate!" she says.

I turn and face her, hoping to connect with her humanity, thinking that it must be harder to shoot someone when you're looking them in the eye. "What do you want, Daisy?" I ask.

*"I said shut up!"* she thunders.

Her eyes dart around the room. She appears unhinged, as if she hasn't slept for days. And like she hadn't really thought this through. Her shaking hands are almost covered by a sweater that's too long for her arms, and she's starting to sweat. She wipes her face with her arm. Maybe she's on something. I don't want to spook her.

I'm a psychologist.

*Almost.*

So, I pretend she's my patient and search my repository for something I can do to calm her. Compliance is all I can think of to buy me time to find a way to take her down or press the panic button, which is up in my bedroom.

"You're going to write a confession," she says.

"A confession to what?" I ask.

"Ryan's murder."

*So that's what this is about.*

"I didn't—"

She points the gun at my chest, and my heart starts pounding even harder. "I wasn't *finished,* Kate," she says in a low rumble through clenched teeth.

"Okay, Daisy," I say.

"And you're going to admit you killed Doug Mitchell and tried to frame me. It's the only way to clear my name."

This isn't the time to tell her she's wrong about Ryan. This isn't the time to show her the video clip of him pushing me to the ground or have her listen to the recording of Ryan saying he never loved her. My only move is to comply with her request and then try to deny it later. If I give her what she wants, she won't kill me.

*I hope.*

"Okay," I say.

"You have paper? And a pen?" she asks.

I fight to suppress a chuckle, but the corners of my mouth lift a bit. This would be comical if I didn't have a gun pointed at my head. Still, it amuses me that she's so unprepared. I wonder if this is some kind of coping mechanism or if I'm losing it.

"You think this is funny, bitch?"

I shake my head and force my face into a frown. "I'm just nervous."

"I asked you a question," she says.

"Upstairs. In my bedroom."

*Where the panic button is located.*

"Let's go," she says, motioning with the gun towards the staircase.

We head up, and I think about spinning around and

knocking her down. But it's too big of a risk. Her finger is on the trigger of a gun.

*Aimed at me.*

Each step feels like an eternity. Like time has stopped dead in its tracks, although we've only been in the house for a few minutes. Finally, we enter my bedroom.

"Where's the paper?" she asks as we stand in the doorway.

My desk sits opposite the doorway, near the foot of the bed. The panic button is over near my nightstand, though, on the opposite side. I need to figure out a way to get over there. Maybe after I write the confession, I can pretend to feel faint and ask to lie down.

"In there," I say. "I have paper in the top drawer. And there're pens in the holder."

"Don't touch a thing," she says.

I nod.

"Sit." Her head juts towards the chair in front of the desk. "Hands on the tabletop." She opens the desk drawer, takes out a sheet of paper, and places it on the desktop. Then, she selects a pen from the holder and hands it to me.

"Now write exactly what I say," she says.

"Okay," I reply.

*I killed my husband, Ryan Breslow, because he was having an affair with Daisy Parker.*

My hands tremble, and I mess up his name. Suddenly, it's not so amusing. I have to cross it out and start again with a new sheet of paper. I'm hoping she won't go ballistic on me.

"Sorry," I say. "I'm a little shaken up."

"Good. You should be." She jabs me in the back with the barrel of her gun, and I flinch. "Keep writing."

*I ran him off the road the night he asked me for a divorce.*

"He didn't ask me for a divorce, Daisy. Is that what he told you?"

I know I should comply with her request and shut my mouth, but I can't help myself. Ryan's having the last laugh, and I can't let that happen. She doesn't stop me, so I continue.

"He told me he was going to break it off with you. Daisy. He was lying to both of us. He wasn't the man you thought he was."

"Shut up, Kate! You're the liar! And I'll kill you if you say another word."

But I notice a slight, almost imperceptible shift in her tone. Maybe I have a shot at reasoning with her.

She continues.

*Then, I killed Doug Mitchell and framed Daisy Parker to punish her for the affair.*

"I was having an affair with Doug Mitchell, Daisy. We were in love. We were planning to double-cross Claudia and leave for New York. Why would I do that?" I ask.

"Write it!" she hisses. "I don't care if you did it or not. I'm not going down for it."

Then she hits me on the side of the head.

*Hard.*

Not with the gun. With her open palm. My head swirls, and my fear is replaced with a simmering rage fueled by the pain.

I turn my head to look at her. "Was that really necessary? I was just about to sign this."

"No! We're not done yet," she says. "Don't sign it. Turn around and write what I say, or I swear I'll blow your brains out."

"Fine," I say. But the compliant tone in my voice is gone.

She continues.

*I'm sorry for all that I've done, and I can no longer live with the guilt.*

Then it hits me.

This is a suicide note.

*She's planning to kill me.*

To hell with reasoning with her. With nothing to lose, I crouch down and shove the chair back into her with all my might. She falls back, taking me with her.

A shot rings out.

*Have I been hit?*

I don't think so.

I have no idea if she's still holding the gun or if she dropped it. She's wedged between the floor and the chair, and I'm on top of her, suddenly aware of the searing pain in my left shoulder, which took the brunt of the impact. She grabs at me, digging her nails into the flesh of my forearm. She's surprisingly strong. I can't stay like this forever. She pushes me up and off the chair. I roll to my right, closer to my night-stand. I didn't see the gun, and I'm hoping maybe it went flying somewhere. If I knew where the gun was, I'd go for it, but I don't—and hopefully neither does she.

In a split-second decision, I spring up and hurl myself towards my nightstand, hoping that if I press the panic button and the alarm starts blaring, she'll see that it's in her best interest to abort this insane plan and make a run for it. I leap onto the bed, roll over it, and land on the ground. A jolt of pain shoots through me. I'm still an arm's length from my nightstand, and I can't quite reach it.

I whip my head around.

Daisy's right in front of me.

And someone is behind her.

*Holding the large metal vase from my hallway high above her head.*

It comes crashing down on her skull with a thundering thud and terrifying cracking sound that can only mean one thing. Daisy's eyes roll back into her head, and she drops to the floor.

Margaret stands before me with a triumphant look on her face, holding the heavy vase in her hands. She drops the vase and bends down to check on Daisy as blood pours out of the crevices in her skull. I grab my phone to get help.

"Oh my god, Margaret. She was going to kill me," I say, turning from her and reaching for my cell on the nightstand. "I'll call an ambulance."

"Not so fast, Kate," Margaret says. "Don't touch that phone. We need to get our stories straight."

I turn back to her, and my eyes nearly pop out of my head.

Margaret's holding Daisy's gun in her hands.

*And she's pointing it at me.*

"Well," Jesse says. "There's not much more for me to do here, so I'll probably be headed back to Detroit tonight. I can run down the leads from anywhere."

Jesse's efforts to find someone with access to Daisy Parker's apartment have turned up nothing as of yet. Ditto for Sloane's mission to find footage of anyone close to this case in Saugatuck, although she's giving it another try today. Jesse's sitting across the table from Travis in the conference room of the precinct, going through the case one last time, and he realizes that her presence unnerves him. He's never been one to relive the past, and her visit is stirring up feelings that no longer serve his needs.

"Probably time to get back to that family of yours," he says. "I'm sure you're missed."

She lets out a sigh. "My older one's at a weird stage. She's eight. Two years ago, I was her hero. Now I can't do anything right. It's like she hates me. Of course, she adores her father."

Travis could not possibly care less about this sort of thing, and it dawns on him that he's not the least bit interested in getting to know someone else's kids, even for someone as special as Jesse once was. But if he crosses single moms off the list, he'll eliminate probably eighty percent of the women in his age group.

"Travis. There's something I need to tell you," Jesse says.

"What's that, Jess?"

"We're considering a trial separation. Things have been . . . tense."

His eyes widen. "Tense? Are you in any danger?" Travis asks.

"Oh, no! Nothing like that," she says. "Goodness, no." Jesse shakes her head and then lets out a breath.

He nods. "Good."

An awkward silence fills the space between them.

"But I've been thinking a lot lately. About us," she says, a hint of hesitation in her eyes.

"Well, that's only natural, considering you're here with me. Just your luck, getting stuck with this assignment. It'll fade when you go home."

"If I'm being honest, I asked for this assignment," she reveals.

Travis swallows. "I see."

"I wanted to see you again, and when this case popped up . . ."

"Look, Jess. I see where this is going. Go back to your husband. Or don't. But I'm not giving you a soft landing. You've got kids. Try to work it out if you can. Nothing's changed here. I haven't changed."

"Maybe I have."

"I doubt it. People don't change. Not when it comes to

things like that. We gave it our best shot, Jess, and it didn't work. There's a reason for that," he says.

From the look on her face, it wasn't the response she was hoping for, but it's the only one he can give her.

A call comes in.

*Thankfully.*

Saving him from this awkward conversation.

He picks up.

"We've got a problem," Travis says.

"What's up?"

"Dispatch said a patrol car's headed to Kate Breslow's house. Something about a disturbance."

"Any idea what's going on?" Jesse asks.

"No idea. I'll need to head over there," Travis says. "My best guess is Daisy Parker's resurfaced," he says.

"I'll go with you," she says.

They rush out of the precinct and hop in his car, and he's back in his element.

*Doing what he was meant to do.*

# CHAPTER 32
## KATE

"Margaret? What's going on?" I'm so stunned I can hardly get the words out of my mouth. Blood is splattered across her face and hair, and she's shaking like a leaf. The shock I felt a moment ago gives way to nausea, and I feel like I'm going to throw up.

"How could you do this to me, Kate?" Margaret says, as her voice breaks. "After all I've done for you?"

"I don't under—"

"You're leaving me! You think I wouldn't find out?" Tears are pooling in her eyes, about to run down her cheeks. She's not so much pointing the gun at me now. More like waving it around, which might be even worse.

I can reach the panic button, but I don't dare press it. If it starts blaring, it might spook her. "Oh, Margaret. I'm so sorry. I was going to tell you tomorrow at lunch. Remember? We were meeting for lunch."

"I treated you like a daughter, Kate. And this is the thanks I get? I guess you were using me. Until you could get out of here and go back to your *real* friends, back in New York."

"Margaret. It's not like that," I say. "I have nobody back in New York."

*Then, the guilt hits me.*

Because she's right, I have taken her for granted. I knew it would upset her if I left, which is why I'd been avoiding that conversation. But I never thought she'd snap like this.

Meanwhile, Daisy's bleeding out all over my bedroom floor, and if there's any chance we can save her, we have to move fast. I don't want another death on my conscience.

"I need to press the panic button and get help, Margaret. We have to check on Daisy and call an ambulance. To protect both of us. It's what we're required to do. Even if you did this to stop her from killing me. Can you please put the gun down?"

"She's gone, Kate."

"We have to try," I say, although it's pretty clear she's right about that.

"Don't you see? We can pin it on her," she says. "Jealous mistress. It's perfect."

"What are you talking about?"

"Ryan's murder."

*Then it hits me.*

The terrifying truth reveals itself to me.

"Margaret? What have you done?"

"I did it for you, Kate. To protect you. Nobody was there to protect me from Marty. I couldn't let that happen to you. I saw Ryan for what he was. I was there that night, in the parking lot. When he snapped at you."

"It was you?" My voice is barely above a whisper.

She grits her teeth. "I wasn't going to let him get away with it. I followed him. At first, to see what he would do. But I got madder and madder. I started driving faster and faster.

And before I knew it, I was right on his tail. He lost control and went over the edge. I'm not sorry, though. He would have killed you, Kate. What were you thinking, giving him an ultimatum like that? You should have come to me."

"I tried. I drove past your house that night," I say.

"But I wasn't there," she says. Her hand goes to her forehead. "What have I done?"

"Let me call an ambulance, Margaret."

A teardrop escapes and trickles down her face. She wipes it away with her free hand, but she's still got the gun in the other one. "Wait. There's more."

My stomach lurches. "Doug? Margaret, you didn't . . ."

"No. I didn't kill him," she says. "But I planted those panties on his boat a while back. I found them in *your* house. I cleaned up *their* mess to spare you the pain. I knew you were having an affair with Doug and that it would come back to haunt you if anyone found out, especially Claudia. So, I planted them on Doug's boat to confuse people. In case your affair ever came to light. If they found out about the affair, it would be bad for you. They were already suspicious of you for what happened to Ryan. That's why I took your burner phone."

"Then you put it back," I say. "When you realized that it could help clear me."

She nods, and I don't want to think about how many times she must have let herself into my home. Was that the presence I felt? I think back to the keypad conversation when she warned me that someone could see me punch in the numbers. Had I also inadvertently given her the code to the alarm? Or did she come in during the day before I put it on in the evening?

The gun is tilted slightly to her right, away from me. I

think about going for it, but it's too risky for both of us. There's still a chance I can talk her down.

"We have to call for help, Margaret."

"No!" she cries out. "Blame it all on me. I'm a goner anyway, Kate. I'm sick. A type of blood cancer. It's fatal. I don't have much time left."

I'd noticed that she'd lost some weight, and I didn't even think to ask her about her health. I've been so self-absorbed.

*Is that why she was busy all week?*

*Doctor's appointments?*

"Margaret, I'm so sorry."

"You've got your whole life ahead of you, and you don't need this scandal hanging over your head. Old people like me are dispensable. *Invisible.* It's my last gift to you. Tell them everything I told you. Record my confession if you want. Tell them I killed both of them and get on with your life."

She turns the gun on herself.

"No! Margaret. Please!" My voice quivers. "Don't do it."

She closes her eyes and places the barrel of the gun against her temple. I'll never be able to live with it if she kills herself. This will haunt me forever. And suddenly, it's as if all the pain I've been shielding myself from over the years hits me all at once, like a gut punch. The people I took for granted. My mom, before she died. Then my dad. My grandmother. My entire family. The ones you *can* take for granted in your life because they love you unconditionally. All gone.

*Who would shed a tear for me if I died right now?*

"Please!" I cry out.

"Why Kate? Give me one reason I shouldn't end it right now."

"Because I need you, Margaret. You're all I have, too."

Her eyes open, a spark of hope peeking through the anguish.

"And I'll take you with me," I say.

We stare at each other for a few long moments. Then she drops the gun, and I press the panic button, realizing that we'll have to lie a little about the timeline.

Margaret begins to weep as the alarm blares. Then it hits me, too. A gut-wrenching wave of grief wells up from deep in my core, erupting into a guttural sob that twists my insides, spasm after spasm releasing the tension as I gasp for breath. Knowing we have to move fast, I force myself to shut down my emotions. Pulling myself together, I call for an ambulance.

*Then we make a plan.*

———

"Take me through this one more time," Whittaker says.

We're in my living room. I've been through this once with him and once with Special Agent Carver. I know better than to cop an attitude, though. I do as I'm told and go through it once more, hoping I don't mix up any of the details.

"Daisy forced her way into the house," I say. "She held a gun to my head." My security tape confirmed this.

*Thankfully.*

"Then she had me disarm the system."

Adjusting the ice bag on my shoulder, I explain how she forced me upstairs, leaving out the part about my nervous chuckle, which could have gotten me killed.

"She wanted me to write a suicide note, claiming that I'd run Ryan off the road that night. And that I'd killed Doug and planted her underwear to frame her. She said she wanted to clear her name. She was shaking, like maybe she was on drugs or something."

I continue, and I'm doing fine because it's all true. The part about our scuffle. Margaret arriving. The metal vase crashing down on Daisy's head. Her body dropping to the floor.

*Then I get nervous.*

*This is the tricky part.*

"Remind me. How did Margaret get in your house?"

"The door was open," I say.

"It doesn't lock automatically?"

"No. It doesn't."

"Did you hear a knock?" he asks.

"Um, no," I say.

"Was Margaret in the habit of walking into your home unannounced?"

*Apparently.*

"No. She said she heard Daisy yelling at me. My bedroom window was open."

"There's about a three-minute delay between the time you pushed the panic button and the time you called for an ambulance," Whittaker notes.

"Yes. We were both in shock, I think. Margaret bent down to see if Daisy was still alive. I was frozen to the spot for a bit, trying to process everything that had happened."

He nods, seeming to accept my story. Then Whittaker leaves me sitting in the living room to head upstairs and process the crime scene. The medical examiner has just arrived, and I'm comforted by the fact that she won't find anything that conflicts with what I've already told him.

But Margaret and I barely had time to get our stories

straight, and I can only hope she's keeping it together. They've separated us, and I need to talk to her.

*Alone.*

I've got so many questions, and I'm still trying to piece together all that she told me. She ran Ryan off the road, she said. The night I confronted him at the restaurant. And she planted the underwear on the boat. I still have no idea who drugged Doug. Or who, if anyone, pushed him off the side of his boat. Or how his Sundancer came to be docked in Saugatuck.

One thing is certain, though, and a wave of relief floods over me as the information sinks in. All this time, I'd convinced myself that Ryan had killed himself that night after I'd backed him into a corner by threatening to expose him if he didn't pack up and leave.

*And that it was my fault.*

I knew that it was a possibility. I'd read the studies on narcissism and suicide. And if I'm being honest, a part of me hoped to push him in that direction. It was an easy fix to my problems. What kind of therapist wishes someone dead? It's something I'll have to live with because I'll never tell a soul about it.

It wasn't only the guilt that plagued me. I thought that someone might figure it out. I'd read about a case where a woman was convicted of manslaughter for encouraging her suicidal boyfriend to kill himself. I worried that Whittaker would confiscate my computer and see that I'd downloaded those studies and done a paper on narcissistic mortification.

I know it would have been nearly impossible to connect those dots to make a criminal case, but with Daisy poking around, there could have been the makings of a wrongful death suit. Now, I don't have to worry about her or any of it coming to light, and for that, I'm thankful. She would have killed me, I'm sure of it, and I'm not going to lose any sleep over what happened to her. With the guilt for Ryan's death off my shoulders and my house sold, it's time to finally move on and put this place behind me.

*Except for Margaret, that is.*

I made a promise to her. And I'm going to make good on that and take care of her until the end.

# CHAPTER 33
# KATE

So far, it seems as if we've gotten away with it, but it's only been a week. I offered to take a lie detector test, and so did Margaret. We both passed—because everything we told them was the truth. The part about Daisy forcing herself into my house. The part where she made me draft a suicide note. The part about Margaret saving me from getting shot to death and never leaving this house alive.

I believe Margaret when she says she didn't have anything to do with Doug's death, and with the mystery of the red panties solved, my money's on Claudia or one of the Mitchells for the murder. I'd like to get justice for Doug, but not now. Margaret offered to confess about planting the underwear, but I talked her out of it. It would only complicate matters. I'm not going to let her spend her last days in prison, not after what she's been through. Perhaps later, after she passes, I'll tell Whittaker the truth.

It seems as if Marty was a monster. Worse than Ryan. And she put up with it.

*For decades.*

"Things were different back then," she told me. "I left my family and friends for him, just like you. That's why I tried to warn you. Gave up on my dreams of becoming a doctor. Before he started to show his true colors, I got pregnant. At that point, there was really no way out for me."

I think back on my observations about her home. Stripped of all signs of masculinity. I was right that she was trying to shield herself from the pain.

*But it was a different kind of pain.*

"Margaret. Did you try to go to the police?" I asked.

"What good would that have done?" she said. "He was well-liked. Connected. He kept his dark side hidden. It was worse when he drank. He quit for a while, and things were better. But then his firm failed, and he took it out on me. But I protected Caroline. He never touched her. I'd have killed him in his sleep and gone to prison before I'd let him touch my girl."

"I'll bet," I said, not calling attention to the fact that she'd killed Ryan to protect me. I would imagine she'd be even more protective of her own flesh and blood.

"What about your daughter, Margaret?" I asked. "Why don't you see her?"

"That's not something I can talk about," she said.

We left it at that.

Margaret's daughter moved to Germany around the time her husband had a heart attack that took his life. He was a German national with a green card, and her daughter has dual citizenship. I wonder if there's a connection there. If one of them had somehow . . . helped him along. Margaret was a chemistry teacher who wanted to be a doctor, and her daughter works in biotech. I'm sure either of them could have figured out a way to slip him something to induce a heart attack and leave no trace of it. I'm not about to pry, though. It's their business, and the less I know about it, the better.

Meanwhile, I'm staying with Margaret over at her place until we leave for New York next week because my house is still a crime scene. She's not selling it yet. She wants to leave it for her daughter and let her decide what to do with it. Lucky for me, my sale was recorded before Daisy was killed. I thought maybe the attorney for the mystery buyer would contact me, looking for some kind of concession, but I haven't heard a word. Perhaps they feel safer, knowing that Daisy Parker's gone and no longer a threat to the neighborhood.

I've settled on Dobbs Ferry as my next stop. It's a quaint village in Westchester, perched on the Hudson, more eclectic and diverse than the others. A quick, twenty-minute train ride into the city. It's close to my externship, and there's an excellent cancer center a few towns away for Margaret. I'm planning to rent first before I buy. With the interest rates where they are, I can siphon off enough to live on without depleting my principal. There's no rush. I've got my whole life ahead of me.

This is both a liberating and a sobering thought. Margaret has about six months to a year, according to the prognosis. I'll need to find another way to fill the void in my life aside from caring for a dying elderly woman. I'm not ready to date again, but perhaps that will change over time. I don't want to give Ryan that much power over me, but I'm not quite there yet.

They say time heals all wounds, but it's not true. Time dulls the pain and allows you to function. But I'd like to do more than just function. I'd like to feel whole again. As soon as I get settled, I'll find a therapist and tackle my emotional baggage.

For now, at least, I'm leaving with my nest egg intact, a nest egg that was bought with my dear father's blood. A triumphant smile spreads across my face as I think about that. My father didn't die in vain. It's a big accomplishment, and I'm rightly proud of myself. Holding my head high, I walk out the front door for the last time.

*And leave Ryan's ghost behind.*

# CHAPTER 34
# TRAVIS

"So where do we go from here?" Sloane asks.

"We keep searching for footage in Saugatuck. Of Daisy Parker, to confirm she killed Doug Mitchell. Or of someone else who shouldn't have been there that day."

With Kate Breslow cleared and leaving town, they moved the Ryan Breslow hit-and-run to the cold case files with no objections from the victim's mother. Travis finds that odd, and he wonders if his mother somehow knows she raised a monster.

They could do the same with the Mitchell case. It's what the higher-ups want. They've spent a lot of time and money on this case. Daisy Parker trying to murder Kate Breslow wraps it up pretty nicely. She killed Ryan Breslow and Doug Mitchell. Tried to blame it on Kate out of jealousy, and then kill her, too. Plus, if they spent time gathering evidence to prove the case, there'd be nobody to prosecute. He's convinced them to leave the case open a bit longer, though, because he's not ready to give up yet and chalk it all up to Parker, as tempting as that might be.

"What do you think happened?" Sloane asks.

"I don't want to speculate until we have more information."

They sit with that for a few minutes. It's a slow day, and he misses the action of the past few months.

"You never did tell me what Margaret Brenner meant the other day. She said she'd done you a favor once. Given the circumstances, I'd like an explanation. I wouldn't want to think that little act of mercy was clouding your judgment."

She's got a smirk on her face, but Travis senses she's not joking. He went easy on Margaret, and the prosecutor's office cleared her of any wrongdoing regarding Daisy's death pretty quickly, with his blessing.

"Come on. You know me better than that," Travis says. "But if you must know, she caught me cheating. On her chemistry final exam."

"Really? And she let you off the hook?"

"Yeah. Gave me a lecture about honesty and second chances. But I never told her the real story."

"So, what's the real story?"

"I took the blame for someone else. Someone cheated off me, not the other way around. Our answers were the same, but I took the fall. She was Margaret's favorite. She never would have believed me anyway."

"You let a girl cheat off of you?"

He shrugs. "Cutest girl in the class. And even after all that, she went to senior prom with another guy."

"Well, that explains your fear of commitment."

Travis laughs, a hearty belly laugh that he hasn't heard emanate from himself in far too long. It feels good. He and

Jesse laughed, he recalls, at least in the beginning. It's hard to laugh when you're alone so much. "Maybe you're onto something there, Sloane. It all goes back to high school chemistry class. You should've been a shrink."

He doesn't tell her what else he noticed that day. Faint bruising on Margaret's face and wrist. He asked her about it, and she chalked it up to being a klutz. But he always had his doubts about Marty Brenner and what was really going on behind closed doors in that household.

So, after the incident with Daisy Parker, he did some digging. Margaret's medical records confirmed what he'd suspected. There were too many ER visits. Far too many accidents. Nobody was that much of a klutz. And if she ran Ryan Breslow off the road to protect another victim of domestic abuse, or if she encouraged Kate Breslow to do so herself, he's not going to lose any sleep over it. He doubts that either of them murdered Doug Mitchell, and he'll keep that case front and center. The Mitchell family isn't getting off that easily because he still feels that Claudia and Gavin Mitchell are the most likely perpetrators as far as Doug Mitchell is concerned.

In the meantime, he needs to get a life. Seeing Jesse made him realize what he'd been missing. The touch of a woman. The delightful trill of a feminine laugh. Someone with no baggage, though. And preferably no kids. Or at least none under the age of twenty.

It's worth a try, so he pulls up a dating app and signs up. Then he grabs a cold case folder from a decade ago. A missing person's case he checks in on now and again. He spends a good ten minutes on it, and nothing jumps out at him, so he puts it aside.

His phone pings, and he turns it over. A few women have

already hit him up, and he thinks twice about the dating app idea. Seems a little desperate, to contact him so fast.

Then a call comes in.

A robbery in the high-rent district.

"Finally!" he says.

"Flip you for it," Sloane says.

"Heads, I win. Tails you lose." He flashes her a cheeky grin.

She rolls her eyes. "Just go, Travis," she says.

*And he does.*

# EPILOGUE

## ONE YEAR LATER

"Do you need anything else?" I ask. "Want a sip of tea?"

Margaret nods.

I bring the teacup, razor-thin with tiny flowers and a gold rim, to her lips. A few drops of tea moisten them, but she can't quite swallow. The liquid dribbles down her chin. I dab it with a napkin.

"Nothing like a good cup of tea." Her voice is raspy, barely above a whisper.

"In a proper porcelain cup," I add.

"You've learned, Kate." She forces a smile.

"Yes, I have," I say.

"Hello?" a voice calls out.

"There's someone here to see you," I say.

Her daughter walks into the room, and for a moment, Margaret looks puzzled. Then, her face lights up. "Caroline," she says. "But you shouldn't—"

"Shh, Mom. It's okay," her daughter says, holding a finger to her lips.

She walks over to her mother, and they join hands. A tear runs down Margaret's face. There's a slight resemblance, but Caroline's coloring is darker. Almost Eastern European, unlike Margaret, who looks Irish.

Like me.

*Kate Sullivan.*

I smile.

Taking my name back felt great.

They huddle together, drinking in the sight of each other after all these years. I excuse myself, giving them their privacy.

After twenty minutes or so, Caroline joins me in the waiting room of the hospice facility.

"She's sleeping," Caroline informs me.

"Gamma sleeping," Lily says.

I bounce Lily on my lap. She giggles in that silly, delightful way that toddlers do. It tugs at my heartstrings every time I hear it.

"I didn't realize you had a child," Caroline says.

"She's not my child. Well, not yet, anyway."

I explain that I decided to become a foster parent after Margaret went into long-term care. I'd started dating again, trying to fill the void, but I realized that I wasn't ready. My therapist suggested adoption, but that seemed like too big of a commitment. This was a good compromise, and I've gotten so attached to Lily that I'm trying to make it permanent. It's a complicated situation, though, so I need to manage my expectations.

"How old is she?" Caroline asks.

"Almost two," I say.

"She's adorable."

I offer her a polite smile. Saying thank you doesn't seem quite right. I had nothing to do with how she looks.

"How long can you stay?" I ask. "She doesn't have much longer. It'll be any day now. You got here just in time."

"I can stay until the end," Caroline says. "Thanks so much for contacting me."

"Of course."

"But Kate? There's something my mother asked me to do. After she passes."

She shows me a letter.

It's hand-addressed.

*To Detective Travis Whittaker.*

"It absolves you of—"

I hold up my hand. "Don't say anything more. I don't want to know, Caroline. Do whatever she wants," I say.

Caroline nods. "After she passes, I'll send it. Right after she passes. I'm afraid I'm exhausted," she says. "I flew all night. I need to get going."

"Go. Get some sleep. We'll stay a while longer and then head out."

When I enter Margaret's room, she's fast asleep. I think about what that letter means. Did she confess to all of it? Or just to planting the underwear? And how will it impact me?

Maybe it will all come out. What Margaret did to protect me from Ryan. Whatever the two of them may have done to get rid of Marty Brenner. Or maybe that part of the story will die with Margaret.

I'm not going to try to stop her. It gives me relief, knowing that justice might still be served in Doug's murder, and whatever happens from there is out of my hands. If I'm somehow held accountable for my role in covering up the truth, then so be it.

I notice that Margaret's not taking any breaths. I call for the nurse and wait for her to arrive. She confirms my suspicions. The doctor comes in a few minutes later and calls time of death.

"Gamma sleeping," Lily says.

I smile at the beautiful little girl with the brunette ringlets balanced on my hip.

"Yes, Lily. Grandma's sleeping. "Now, let's go home."

———

Claudia Mitchell takes in the shoreline of Lake Michigan, letting her Sundancer drift around in the currents. She takes in the sight of her homes, high above the bluff, and she has to admit, the revetment wasn't a bad idea. It seems to have done the trick, and now that she and Sam Bolger own six of the ten homes on the bluff, they've been able to change the setback regulations, preserving her family home for the time being.

"Hey, hon," she says to Sam. "You want another beer?" She's reclining on one of the boat's loungers, and Sam's next to her.

Sam shakes his head. "No. I think we should head back. I don't like the look of that cloud." He sits up as if he's about to rise and points to the western sky. "And the wind's picking up."

"You worry too much," she replies. "Ten more minutes? Please?" She places a hand on his and then removes it.

He leans over and gives her a peck on the lips. "You know I can't say no to you, Madame President." He reaches into the cooler, pops open a can of Heineken, takes a sip, then leans back on the lounger and looks over at her.

"Ten more minutes, but then we head back." He pats her hand, then takes another sip of his beer.

Sam adores her, and that feels good. She appreciates him and his companionship. And the fact that he stepped down from his position as town council president when she wanted the job. But she'll never love anyone the way she loved Doug.

That's why his betrayal stung so much. She started this affair with Sam in retaliation, but it did little to alleviate her pain. So, when Doug had refused to break it off with Kate and insisted on backing her shoreline plan, adding insult to injury, she couldn't let him get away with it.

She tells herself that she never planned for Doug to die. She tried her best to talk him out of backing Kate, even promising to go easy on him in the divorce if he gave her what she wanted as far as the shoreline. But he refused to grant her even that small concession.

So, she dosed his cocktail canister with a few ground-up tablets of Estazolam she'd snatched from a friend's medicine cabinet, thinking that Doug would fall asleep and miss the meeting. Figuring that with Sam's help, the vote could still go her way, and then she could preserve her family home, divorce Doug, and screw him to the wall.

After Doug left that day for the dock, she called Sam to let him know that she hadn't been able to talk him out of supporting Kate's plan and that Doug was going to betray the both of them and vote Kate's way. She didn't tell him about slipping Doug the drugs because she wasn't sure yet if she could fully trust him. She told him about Doug going out for a spin on the lake, though.

"Don't worry about it," he said. "I'll go talk to him. You leave it to me."

When Doug didn't show up back home that afternoon,

she called the police. She didn't connect the dots right away, but later she did. She knows Sam was at the dock that day because she drove there herself, having had second thoughts about the drugs. But when she saw Sam in the parking lot walking towards the dock, she decided to do as he said and leave it all to him.

In her private moments, she visualizes what might have happened out on the lake that day. She tells herself it was an accident and that Sam only went there to try to change Doug's mind. Perhaps he and Doug got in a scuffle, and Doug went overboard. Or maybe Sam was below deck, and Doug fell in and drowned because of the drugs she gave him.

Now Doug's gone, and nothing she can do will change that, so she pushes all that ugliness out of her mind. Because it's worked out so well for her. If she'd divorced him, he'd have gotten away with some of her assets, even with the prenup. Now, the money's all hers, as well as the proceeds from his life insurance policy.

*It serves him right.*

*He should have been more reasonable.*

She finds it romantic how far Sam's willing to go to make her happy, keeping whatever happened out on the lake that day to himself and shielding her from any danger. That's what a man should do. Protect his woman. And for that, she's grateful.

She reaches for him, suddenly hungry for his touch.

"Later. We need to get going," he says.

The boat tilts.

Abruptly.

*Violently.*

The Sundancer rises like they're going up in an elevator. Claudia's stomach lurches, and she grabs Sam's arm in a panic. Dark clouds sweep in, and a bolt of lightning flashes across the sky.

"Wait here," he commands.

Sam rushes towards the cockpit, and a deafening, roaring sound fills her ears. Claudia springs up and tries to make her way to Sam. She stumbles, almost falling off the deck. Grabbing the rail, she holds on for dear life.

"Holy shit!" Sam calls out as he looks out on the lake.

He throws her a life jacket.

"What's happening?" Claudia cries out. Her westward view is blocked by the boat's cockpit. She looks back towards the shoreline. Wave after wave batters the fragile bluff, and a giant piece of earth in front of her family home breaks off, crashing to the shore.

"Put this on! *Now!*" Sam barks.

Fumbling with the mechanism, Claudia starts to panic. Her vision narrows, and she feels as if she might pass out.

"I can't do it, Sam. I'm shaking."

Sam jumps down from the cockpit, rushes over to her, and secures it. Then he grabs the other one and jams his arms through the holes.

"Hurry, Sam!" she pleads.

But she can see that it's too late for Sam. Before he can fasten his life preserver, the boat tilts on its side. They're holding on, barely, as the boat writhes and gyrates in the angry waters.

Then a massive wall of water rises from the surface, sucking back everything in its path. Sam's jacket dangles from his arm for a moment before slipping off him. Their screams fill the air as the massive wave rises over them.

*And it swallows them whole.*

# ACKNOWLEDGMENTS

I want to thank the many individuals who helped with this novel. First, my sincere thanks to Josh W. Packer, Special Agent in Charge, CGIS Central Field Office, whose expert advice allowed me to accurately portray the complicated and complex web of state, local, and federal agencies that have jurisdiction over the Great Lakes communities. I cold-called Josh out of the blue one morning from Honolulu and left a hesitant message explaining who I was and why I was calling. He was gracious enough to not only return my call that day, but to schedule another one with me, a rather lengthy one, to explain what Coast Guard Investigative Services (CGIS) does as well as give me tips about how a homicide investigation might work if it happened out on Lake Michigan. His expertise and generosity with his time went a long way towards crafting a believable yet intriguing mystery on the Great Lakes.

I would also like to thank William Hoffman, retired US Coast Guard Chief Petty Officer in Honolulu, who first clued me in to the fact that there was such an entity as CGIS and also shared with me some of the life-threatening situations that happen out in the waters on a regular basis. He also brainstormed some hypotheticals with me, which was very valuable. The Coast Guard truly does just that: guards our coasts from myriad dangers and threats on a daily basis, and it was my pleasure to shed some light on what they do.

Also, *The Life and Death of the Great Lakes* by Dan Egan was a fascinating read that provided a great deal of information on the history of the lakes from an environmental as well as economic perspective, providing great background information for my novel and allowing me to geek out on some fascinating detail, most of which did not make it into the novel. If you like that sort of thing, check out his book. I'd also like to thank my dear friend Debbie, a bestie of mine since middle school, who shared her expertise about shoreline revitalization and opened her home to me so I could see a shoreline revitalization plan in action. My descriptions of Lake Michigan, its magnificence and its dangers, are accurate. It's almost as treacherous as an ocean—minus the sharks and jelly fish—but commanding the same amount of respect from boaters, beachgoers, and residents. My story, however, is purely from my imagination. For more information about the warning signs of abusive relationships, see the National Domestic Violence Hotline, at thehotline.org. They can be reached 24/7 at 1-800-799-SAFE, or text START to 88788.

As always, I'd like to thank my alpha and beta readers: Donna, Robin, Susan, and my husband, who helped me fine tune the plot and deepen my character development. Thanks to my ARC readers on various sites who take time to download and review my books, and to the influencers on various social media sites who take time to promote my books. Thanks to Christina Yother who did an amazing job editing and proofreading my manuscript, while also offering excellent suggestions on how to deepen the story and bring it to life. Many thanks to fellow thriller authors Leslie Lutz, R.G.

Belsky, and Tracey Devlyn for their support and encouragement.

Thanks to my readers who support my writing by buying my books, taking time to review my books, and encouraging me to keep writing. It's not an easy undertaking, writing a novel, but when I hear from someone that they read and enjoyed it, it truly makes my day. I read all my reviews, and they help me to improve, so please keep them coming. I appreciate it.

I'm presently finish up a new mystery where a romantic getaway takes an unexpected turn. Look for *A Little Getaway* sometime in late 2024. For information on new releases, special deals, and book recommendations, sign up for my mailing list. While you're there, be sure to download my free novelette, *Stark Justice: A Honolulu Cold Case*, part of my Hudson Valley Series, at www.bonnietraymore.com.

# ABOUT THE AUTHOR

Bonnie Traymore is the award-winning, Amazon charts international bestselling author of six domestic suspense thrillers. Her books feature strong but relatable female protagonists who find themselves in extraordinary circumstances. Originally from the New York City area, she's lived in Honolulu with her family for the last few decades but travels regularly. She's also an accomplished non-fiction writer, historian, and veteran educator with a doctorate in United States History. She has taught at top independent schools in Honolulu, Silicon Valley, and New York City, and she's taught history courses at Columbia University and the University of Hawai'i.

Please enjoy a sample of
*The Stepfamily: A Psychological Thriller*
Book 1 of my Silicon Valley Series

# PROLOGUE

She stands in silence, reading the weathered letter she holds in her trembling hands—over and over and over. A rage simmers deep inside her, about to erupt as she grasps the implications. Yet it all makes perfect sense for her now. The pieces of her life that never quite fit together suddenly snap into place as the truth reveals itself to her.

Her entire life, she now realizes, has been a lie. A fraud. A fractured fairy tale. How can anyone be expected to turn a blind eye to that kind of realization? How can anyone forgive that level of deception?

She's trying to hold it together, she really is, but the feeling bubbling up inside her is too powerful to suppress. It washes over her like a tidal wave, and suddenly she's willing to risk everything to get what she needs—and eliminate anyone who stands in her way.

# CHAPTER ONE

I've never felt at home in this family because it's not really mine. But I try. Why? I don't really know. I could speak up. I could protest. I could leave. But I don't.

My husband is tenser than usual this morning. I can see it in his jawline when he walks into the kitchen.

"How's the approval coming?" I ask.

"Oh, you know, the usual hurdles. Nothing to worry about," he replies. He tries to hide it, but his discomfort breaks through. His voice is a little singsongy, always a sign that something's up.

He walks over to the coffee pot, pours himself a cup, and pops a slice of bread in the toaster. A dark blue tie hangs loose around his neck. He never wears one. Hardly anyone in Silicon Valley does, so it must be an important day. But for some reason, I don't think his unease has anything to do with work.

"Got a big meeting today?" I ask.

"The board wants an update," Peter replies.

"Aren't you just waiting for the FDA?"

"Yeah."

"So, isn't that the update?"

"Yeah." He smiles. "But you know how they are."

Then he shrugs, and I smile back. He butters his toast and pours some more coffee into a travel mug. I can tell that's all I'm going to get out of him. He's a calm man—most of the time. But he does have a temper, and even after twelve years, I still can't tell what might set it off. I can tell he's stressed, so I leave it alone.

I watch him walk over to the large beveled mirror that hangs in our dining room. He fastens his tie in one fluid motion. It looks sexy. Masculine. Commanding. The way he snaps it up and down at the same time to force it into compliance. He's older than me, but he still gets my heart racing with his salt-and-pepper hair and chiseled physique. His sleeves are rolled up a bit, exposing his muscular forearms.

He walks back to the kitchen and wolfs down his toast. Standing at the island countertop, I continue to make a veggie sandwich to pack for lunch. He places his dish in the sink behind me. We don't speak. It's a comfortable silence, but I can't shake the feeling that something is up.

I turn around to face him. "Well, I'm sure you'll dazzle them." I smile and rest my hand on Peter's bicep. I run my thumb across its taut surface.

"I don't know about that." He places his hand on my shoulder, leans over, and gives me a peck on the lips. "Have a good day." Then he grabs his coffee and heads out the side door to the garage.

I hear his car start and the garage door rise up. We have a two-car garage, but there's only space for one car because he's got all kinds of tools and sports equipment that take up the other half. It was like that when we started dating. Only one car in the garage. Twelve years later, my car still sits in the driveway.

I don't belong here. I'm still a visitor. Just like my car.

———

I'm searching through my clothes rack, second-guessing myself once again. I turn to look at myself in the full-length mirror that hangs on the opposite side of my closet. My navy skirt sits just above the knee, and I worry that people might think I'm playing up my sexy legs. But I'm not. It's just how my legs look. I don't want to wear pants. My blouse is modest, and I tell myself to stop being so insecure. I pull out a few different pairs of shoes from the cubbies and try them on. I land on strappy sandals with a medium heel. They're dark, almost the same color as my hair. I look professional but in a confident, sexy way. It's fine.

I have a big day today too. My career is really taking off. Finally. I was so young when I met Peter. Only twenty-seven. I'd just finished graduate school, a marketing MBA, and at first, there was too much going on in our lives to do much of anything with it. But I've made up for lost time. And I recently got a big promotion. Laura Sato Foster, Vice President of Monetization. Is that what's making him uncomfortable? The fact that I might not need him anymore? He's always been a big supporter of my career. It can't be that. But something is bothering him, that's for sure. He even rejected my advances last night, which he's never done before. He just turned fifty, and I hope it's not a sign of what's to come.

I make my way downstairs and out the front door to the driveway where my car sits. It's a silver Audi A6, so it's not an over-the-top choice, especially for this area, but it's certainly garage-worthy. I plop my satchel in the trunk, and then I notice something. A small stream of fluid is running out from under the car. We live in Los Altos Hills near the top of a long road—a very winding and steep one. Our driveway also slants down a bit; otherwise, I don't think I would have noticed the fluid. Thank goodness for gravity.

I'm a bit neurotic, the kind of person who runs back into the house to make sure the stove is off. I always pump my brakes before I back out of the driveway. Losing brakes on a hill like the one we live on could be fatal, and while that trickle of liquid could be anything, I have a sinking feeling in my stomach.

I open the car door and get behind the wheel. I press the start button and see the brake indicator light up. Then I step hard on the brake pedal. There's a slight resistance at first, but then my foot sinks to the floor. I realize then that it must be the brake fluid—one of my biggest fears. I feel a strange tingling in the back of my head.

I try not to catastrophize, but it's a pretty new car, although it's due to be serviced. Do brake lines start leaking for no reason? Probably not. Even before I call for help, I know this isn't good, and my stomach lurches as I consider the implications. It's quite possible that someone has tampered with my brake line.

*Someone who's out to get me?*

———

Peter's seated at the mahogany conference table at work, but his mind is a mile away. He's trying to forget about the email he found in his spam folder the other day, but it gnaws at him like a tick burrowing into his ankle flesh.

*"Peter?* Are you with us?" the chairman barks.

"Yes!" Peter snaps back into reality. He knows he has to get his head in the game, but he's missed the question completely, so there's no way he can fake it. He can get away with something like that once but not a second time, so he forces himself to focus.

"George asked if you have any concerns about what Sahil's team found when they tried to reproduce the results for the lung cancer experiments." It was the CEO, repeating the chairman's question.

"Sorry, I was looking over the FDA's last response. Yes, of course I have concerns."

"What do you plan to do about it?"

"We've already started on another round of experiments. I'm sure it was their mistake. We've performed those experiments numerous times for the study. They've only done it once, so I wouldn't worry just yet."

"We've already released that data in a preprint," the chairman says. "You better hope it was their mistake."

"Give me a week, okay?"

Everyone nods in agreement. Nobody wants this to be an issue, especially with a lucrative merger and FDA approval of their drug on the horizon. It will be fine. The data is good, he tells himself.

And even if it's not, it's the least of his worries right now.

———

"You look rattled. Is everything okay?" My assistant, Mina, looks up at me as I go rushing past her desk and into my office twenty minutes before my first important meeting as the new Vice President of Monetization—and two hours later than normal.

"Car trouble. I had to take an Uber," I call out to her and duck into my office. I wasn't about to tell anyone at work about the brake line. What if it was one of them?

Mina pokes her head in my door as I toss my half-opened satchel on my desk, spilling the contents onto the surface.

"Car trouble?" She's eyeing me with a curious look, hands on her hips, her dark hair cascading down the front of her tan sweater dress. She seems to sense that something's up, although it's hard to tell with her. She's got these mysterious coal eyes, the eyes of an old soul, with lashes so long they look fake, but she swears they're not. I'd kill for lashes like that.

"Car trouble!" I widen my eyes and shrug to let her know we're moving on. We've had a friendship of sorts over the years, although she's quite a bit younger than me. But now that she's working directly for me, I've had to pull back a bit.

"Do you need anything for the meeting?" she asks.

I smile. "No, I'm good, thanks. Just a few minutes to collect my thoughts." She's a great assistant. I consider telling her about my car, but there's no time.

"I'll leave you to it then." She exits, and I decide I'll probably fill her in on the brake incident later. After I've had time to process it. If there's anyone I can trust around here, it's her.

The mechanic who came out to the house confirmed what I'd suspected. The rubber brake hose had been severed, but he couldn't say for sure that it had been tampered with. It's apparently hard to prove something like that. Sometimes road debris—a sharp rock, for example—could damage it enough to weaken it, and then it could simply rupture. And there's plenty of road debris where I live. I'm looking at a photo taken by the mechanic. There's a smoother-looking break on one side, and then it's ragged on the other like it tore apart. He also said that extreme heat could wear down the rubber more quickly, and we've certainly had our share of that this summer. But I'm not convinced by his road debris theory.

Instead of preparing for my meeting, I Google "brake line cut" and discover that there have been isolated pockets of this sort of vandalism in various communities across the country recently. Phoenix. Denver. The Seattle area. They've all been hit. I play a few videos of news broadcasts and listen to frantic residents recount their stories. Like me, at first, they thought that someone was out to get them until a pattern emerged. Who would want to cut the brake hoses of a bunch of strangers? No arrests have been made in any of the cases so far. Although it's a terrifying thought, that a random vandal is targeting my neighborhood, I suppose it's better than the idea that someone is out to get me specifically. I'll go to the police station and file a report. Right after my meeting.

"Laura?" It's my boss at my office door.

I finally have an office, and I thought it would be great. But it doesn't give me as much privacy as you might expect. Nobody closes their door around here. We're technically allowed to work from home if we want, but it's starting to feel like a bad career move if you actually do it.

"Hi, Bethany."

She's the CFO, and I report to her. It's my job to figure out how to start making money. We're venture-capital funded, like many startups in Silicon Valley, and the funding is drying up for this round. I'm supposed to have ideas about how to monetize our product. That's what they pay me for. I've got a few, and I'm sure they're terrible. But maybe that's how everyone feels. We're all just grasping at straws here.

"Are you ready for the meeting?"

"Sure."

"I'm counting on you, Laura. I went out on a limb for you." She holds up a finger, her eyebrows raised high above her translucent hazel eyes as they peer at me, boring into my skull. They look a little unsettling, framed by her wild red hair, which is especially unruly today. "Don't screw this up."

I nod, and she goes on her way. Nobody tells you this, but the gloves come off the closer to the top you get. All the polite formalities and HR-sponsored platitudes fall by the wayside. And what if I do screw up? Then it's game over. I'm out.

*People would kill for an opportunity like this*, Bethany said, when she told me I'd gotten the promotion.

But they wouldn't.

*Would they?*


*If you enjoyed this sample, please check my website at www. bonnietraymore.com for current retail availability.*